THE SPY
AND THE PRIEST

Which Way to Heaven?

~ ~ ~

THE SPY
AND
THE PRIEST

Which Way to Heaven?

~~~

BLAYNEY COLMORE

ISBN 978-0-9982604-0-2

The Spy and the Priest is available for bulk purchase,
special promotions, and premiums. For information on
reselling and special purchase opportunities, visit the
author's website: www.blogblayney.blogspot.com

Book design by Dede Cummings
DCDESIGN BOOKS
Brattleboro, Vermont

For my sisters
Sylvia and Perry
who have edited and encouraged my writing
over the years.

With sorrow I offer this book to
Sylvia
who had hoped she would live to see it.

With thanks and gratitude I offer it to
Perry
whose diligence made it a much better book.

Michaelmas 2016

THE SPY
AND THE PRIEST

Which Way to Heaven?

~~~

I

Max

MAX HARTMAN shifted his considerable weight from one cheek to the other in his leather Eames chair. Sitting in that chair, sometimes with his feet on the matching footstool, sometimes flat on the floor, was the only place other than in bed he could be comfortable for more than five minutes at a stretch.

Despite five major back operations, a sixth scheduled the next month, he'd felt no relief from the sciatic and lumbar pain. Prescription OxyContin and morphine had made him feel slow and stupid without touching the pain.

Max pulled a Marlboro from the pack on the table next to him, holding it against the previously lighted one.

Jesus, they're going to have to dig pretty deep, he thought, *to find an anesthetist willing to put me to sleep this time. Ten days in intensive care the last time won't provide them with a lot of enthusiasm.*

Max's wife Sandra had long since given up trying to persuade him to quit smoking. "How about at least switching to filtered Marlboros, instead of those unfiltered coffin nails?" she badgered him in one final effort.

"Look, Sandra," he said, eyes narrowed, "I can't even get out of this chair without huge effort. There's almost nothing left that I enjoy. If the Marlboros kill me I'll thank them."

Now as he sat surrounded by his collection of battlefield weapons, the date for his surgery approaching, Max's bravado had begun to wear thin. He thought about the two men who jumped him that night in Tehran, 30 years earlier, when he was delivering counterfeit papers to one of the Shah's Savak men, his job being to get them out of the country before the Revolutionaries executed them.

The beating they gave him was the source of the intractable pain he had now.

He didn't tell the Agency how badly he'd been beaten because he knew they'd remove him from the country, and he had several more guys to get out.

I hope those bastards are rotting in hell? And what about you, Max? Think you'll rot in hell? Maybe. If there is a hell those guys probably don't deserve it any more than you do. All working the same job, just opposing teams.

"In recognition of extraordinary bravery and unsurpassed skill, we honor you with the Intelligence Star, the highest award of the Clandestine Service," the Director said, in the ceremony at Langley several months after he left Tehran.

Afterward Max joked with his colleagues about the Agency taking back the award immediately after it was awarded. "Even when we do good it's a secret."

He considered the machine gun propped on the floor, pointing straight at him. Max never understood nor trusted the kinds of investments his friends talked about. Wall Street struck him as a ruse designed to line the pockets of everyone except the unwitting investor.

Max put his money in assault weapons.

"Sometimes the only way to get money out of the stock market is to take a big loss," he told his friends. "The world always needs more weapons. Their value never goes down."

In the 20 years since he'd retired, Max had collected at least one weapon from every war the United States had ever fought, beginning with the Revolution. He'd never given much thought to how his collection might compare with someone else's, until a journalist friend did some research and told Max he had the most extensive known collection in private hands in existence.

Max liked to swivel in his Eames chair and consider the bazooka in the den. On the far wall were two M-16s he brought back from his time as station chief in Islamabad, where he engineered delivery of weapons to the mujahedeen to use against the Soviets.

Those suckers saw some serious action, he thought to himself with satisfaction. He looked down at his legs, stretched out on the ottoman. *They'll hardly hold me up any more, but they did as much as any pair of legs to persuade the Soviets to get the hell out of Afghanistan. Too bad the idiots in our government couldn't see that walking away from Afghanistan and leaving all those weapons behind, was going to cost us more dearly than anyone imagined.*

"Max!" Sandra called, "don't sleep now or you'll never sleep tonight. Let's have some lunch."

I've got the rest of eternity to sleep.

"Good idea. How about some of your world famous chili, laced with OxyContin?"

"I wish you could figure out something besides that stuff for your pain, Max. It must have lost its oomph by now, and you know it's likely to shorten your life."

"Yeah, well my life is pretty much shot already, and the OxyContin works better than martinis."

"You got a piece in the mail from that boarding school you went to for a couple of years," Sandra said. "Your class is having its 50th reunion in June."

"Hadn't thought about that place since God knows when," he said. "Wonder why they sent that to me; didn't graduate. Money, they all want money. Too bad all mine is tied up in guns. Maybe I'll send them a bazooka."

~~~

II

Andy

"Shit, shit, shit, oh fuck, it hurts!"

"Andy, when are you going to learn to hydrate yourself when you play tennis?" Alice asked.

When are you going to learn it's more helpful to express sympathy, and maybe massage my leg cramps, than offer unsolicited advice? Andy thought, but didn't say, as he ripped off the covers and leapt out of bed, trying to massage a knot the size of a tennis ball on the back of his thigh.

He danced around the room, unable to straighten his cramped leg.

"Nice talk. Too bad your parishioners couldn't be here to take this in," Alice scolded.

"I haven't had parishioners for 20 years, and any of them who would be shocked to hear this would already regard me as a fraud."

The words came in staccato, interrupted by sharp inhales each time the muscle seized up.

"Sorry, Andy," Alice's voice softened, "I know it must hurt like hell. You woke me in the middle of a dream, startled me."

At breakfast later that morning Alice apologized again, this time for the remark about parishioners and Andy's bad language. "That's dirty pool; I think the parishioners who really knew you rather enjoyed your colorful language. You pretty much destroyed the sweet-talking stereotype so many have of clergy."

"Well sometimes I miss the drama parishioners provided, but I sure don't miss all those people feeling free to express their opinions about my language, or what I ate for breakfast. How I dressed.

"But, you know, thinking about it all these years later, it was a pretty fascinating way to have spent those 30 years. What else might I have done that made better use of my eccentricities?"

"Amen to that," Alice said. "And I might have been a little stingy about telling you over those years that you were pretty damn good at it.

"Speaking of a lot of years gone by, I just wonder if it's smart for you to be playing such vigorous tennis at your age? I mean you're playing guys at least 20 years younger. No one else your age is playing singles any more."

"Means there's only one person to embarrass me, instead of three. My goal is to drop dead on the tennis court."

"You might want to give yourself a few more years."

"That's what we all say, isn't it? Don't mind dying, but not today. Well today's as good as any day."

"Big talker," Alice retorted. "I bet you'll cower like all the rest of us when the time comes."

"No doubt, but at least I'm not driving myself nuts in the meantime, joining the search for some magic illusion to postpone it."

Alice laughed. "Your parishioners hoped you were privy to esoteric secrets. Might reassure them that maybe they couldn't live forever, but at least they wouldn't be dead forever."

Andy smiled. "I guess we all hear and see what we want. I never understood the eternal life thing. Why would anyone want to live forever? One lifetime is plenty."

"Speaking of living forever," Alice said, "I saw that thing from Salisbury about your class holding its 50th reunion. You planning to go, even though you were there only two years, didn't graduate?"

"Weird, I haven't thought about that school for probably the last 30 of those 50 years. I had no idea they even remembered I'd been there. I haven't had contact with any of those guys. No, I think I can skip it. They're just trying to get me back on the donors' list."

~~~

III

The Penny Drops

A week later Max received an email from Salisbury reminding him of the upcoming class reunion. Included was a list of the members still alive, with email addresses. Max scanned the list, looking for Andy Coffer, his friend from the American School in Manila who had gone to Salisbury with him.

"Holy shit!" he exclaimed. "There he is."

"Who is?" Sandra asked from the next room.

"Andy Coffer, my best friend from seventh grade in Manila and the two years at Salisbury. We were best buddies until we both left Salisbury after sophomore year. Look at this; he's listed as 'The Rev.' I'd never guess he'd end up a priest. Probably gone all prissy and dull. Pity, really a great guy as a kid."

~~~

IV

In The Beginning

Los Baños Prison Camp
Philippines, 1945

"Son, I'm taking you home."

Lt. Ringer from Company B 11TH Airborne Division, his Enfield revolver in his left hand, picked up Max Sampson with his right—"like a sack of potatoes"—as Max would describe it years later—slung the 5-year-old boy onto his hip. He hunched over to stay below the exchange of fire between his own troops and the Japanese, defending against the attack to free American prisoners. He ran as fast as his awkward load permitted, toward an Amtrac where two others from Company B were firing machine guns back at the Japanese defenders.

Max wasn't a lot to carry. He had been starved nearly to death in the three years since he, his parents, and big brother Sam had been arrested just days after the Japanese invaded Manila. From January of 1941 until May of 1943 the Sampsons were held at Santo Tomas, the walled site of the old University of the Philippines. When that camp became overcrowded the Sampsons were moved, along with more than 2,000 others, to Los Baños, the former Filipino agricultural college some 45 miles south of Manila, where their treatment became much more harsh, and the nourishment as sparse as humans can endure and stay alive. More than a third didn't.

Max was a month shy of his second birthday when his life suddenly took this dramatic turn for the worse. His father, a banker with National City Bank of New York, came to the Philippines from New York in 1937, having been told that a tour in Asia would advance his career faster than putting in his time as loan officer back in the States.

Life was good in pre-war Manila. The Sampsons lived in a commodious, bank-owned house, staffed by several servants. The bank paid for a membership at the Manila Polo Club where they mingled with other ex-pats and well-placed Filipinos with whom they did business. Howard Sampson had begun to consider spending his career here. The president of the Manila bank was 10 years older, with ambitions to return to New York and ascend the bank hierarchy. The possibility of succeeding him appealed to Howard. The position included countless perks, including dinner invitations to Malacañang, the presidential palace. It was a far more appealing future to Howard than a corner office and an apartment in New York, navigating internal bank politics.

Several other ex-pats—especially those who had recently fled Shanghai—warned that the Japanese had designs on all of Asia, but Howard and many others considered the Philippines of no great value to the Japanese. What's more, the significant American military presence would discourage the Japanese from challenging an overwhelming force.

Hours after the surprise attack on Pearl Harbor, Japanese aircraft appeared over Manila. Most of the American military was stranded on Cavite and Corregidor. Within 24 hours Manila was declared an open city.

The Sampsons' happy ex-pat life suddenly turned to nightmare, prisoners of the Japanese occupiers.

Max has no memory of life before prison camp. He only vaguely remembers Santo Tomas—he was three and a half when he and his family were moved to Los Baños. Max was a headstrong little boy and his parents had to discipline themselves not to speak of their hatred of their captors within his earshot, for fear he'd do something to put himself in danger. He barely escaped serious injury, or worse, when a sadistic young prison guard, drunk on Saki wine, toyed with him one afternoon, sticking him in the leg with his bayonet.

Max carried the scar on his left leg—and deeper scars in his psyche—for the rest of his life, icons of the vocation that would one day shape his life.

Despite the disciplines he taught himself to erase them, the horrors of life in Los Baños were etched into Max's waking and dreaming memory for life.

~

Lt. Ringer scooped up Max in the chaos of a fire fight. The other prisoners—mostly Americans—weak, sick, starved

nearly to death hadn't the energy to respond to the para-
troopers' shouted commands:

"Run! Stay low!"

Max, while reassured by Lt. Ringer's strong grip, pan-
icked that he'd lost track of his parents and brother.

"Daddy!"

"Don't you worry, son, they're OK, right behind us. We'll
meet them when we get to the truck."

Though he wasn't sure whether to trust this stranger, Max
didn't have the strength to protest. Equally as affecting as his
lifelong memory of the relief he felt when he saw his parents
and brother at the rendezvous point, was of that lieutenant's
strong hold on Max, and his calm, reassuring voice. His
voice would ring in Max's head the rest of his life:

"Son, I'm taking you home."

When he considered the experience years later, and he
often did, he knew he must have been jostled around as Lt.
Ringer ran and dodged, but in his memory it was as if he was
floating, transported on a column of air.

Fifty years later when a French journalist interviewing
Max asked what accounted for the extraordinary choices
he'd made, risking his life many times over in a celebrated
career with the CIA, he told the story of being rescued from
Los Baños by the American lieutenant.

"I thought I owed my life to the country that saved my
life. The sensation of being carried to safety, not only by
an American soldier, but also by some invisible force that
I choose to call God, remains with me every day. Any conscious choice of how to spend the energy given to me has
been directed toward honoring that experience."

~~~

V

In The Beginning

Raleigh, NC 1948
A Dog Dies

Andrew Coffer was training Birdie, his year old, 13-inch-beagle, to heel. Birdie was the whole family's dog, but Andrew—Andy—eight years old, felt ready to assume the responsibility of training Birdie.

He kept her on a short leash by his side, commanding "heel," then letting slack on the lead and, as she wandered off, pulling the leash tight against his leg and sternly repeating "heel." She looked up at him eagerly, tail wagging as Andy leaned down, patted her, and said, "Good girl, Birdie," giving her the kibble reward.

Pleased that she now often responded to his command, even off the leash, Andy was feeling quite accomplished.

One warm summer afternoon he decided to test her at a another level. Birdie was busy at the base of the large, old, oak tree in front of their house, her forepaws up the trunk chasing a squirrel. Andy crossed to the other side of the road, and called, "Birdie, heel!" He wasn't surprised that she didn't respond immediately; after all she was bred for hunting rodents. But he was determined to train her well enough to counter even her instincts.

"Birdie, come, heel!" he shouted again. This time Birdie turned from her squirrel mission, considered Andy, 50 feet away, perhaps remembering the reward that waited, let her paws down from the tree and sprinted for Andy.

At the exact moment that Birdie reached the center of the road, a red Ford Coupe, tires screeching as it raced around the corner, ran over the dog. Andy, paralyzed, watched with a horror he would remember the rest of his life. He hadn't even time to scream before Birdie gave one heart-wrenching cry, the sound of her body thumping piteously beneath the car that was crushing the life out of her. The driver accelerated away.

Andy screamed, Birdie twitched once involuntarily, her entrails smeared on the road. He ran to her, fell on her, guts smearing his face, hair, tasting her blood, sobbing hysterically.

Gertrude, their family maid, though in many ways more mother to Andy than his own, heard the squeal of the tires and Andy's screams. She ran to him, reaching him just as he began to wretch, his vomit mingling with Birdie's blood.

She picked Andy off the dog, murmuring cooing sounds of mourning as Andy clutched Gertrude's neck. She carried him into the house, to the bathroom, stripped off his soiled clothes and put him in the shower. She turned the water on full, paying no mind to getting drenched herself in the process, scrubbed the gore off him.

Andy's sobbing continued, inhaling water streaming into his face, choking, coughing.

"Birdie's gone to Jesus," were the first words Andy remembered hearing from Gertrude. "She's OK now," Gertrude said. In his memory her voice seemed more singing than speaking. "You don't need to worry about her now."

She turned off the water, vigorously rubbed him with the rough side of the towel. Gertrude carried him naked to his room, pulled clean clothes from his bureau and dressed him. Andy hadn't had anyone else dress him in years, would normally be embarrassed for Gertrude to see him naked. Not now. Later he thought Gertrude's tending him may have been all that kept him from falling into some nameless abyss. Nameless, until years later, in seminary, he read scholars in the matter of the fine line that separates life from death, sanity from madness.

She carried him to the telephone in the hall, looked up a number. Still holding him in one arm as if he weighed nothing, she dialed. "I need to talk to Rev. Spencer, it's an emergency." Then, "Rev. Spencer, this is Gertrude at the Coffers. You need to come right away. It's an emergency."

Andy had no sense how long it was between that call and The Rev. Thomas Spencer bursting through the front door without knocking. What he remembered was that his feet never touched the ground between Gertrude pulling him off Birdie's mangled body, and sometime later, when Andy's mother finally arrived home, and Mr. Spencer left.

When he often spoke of it, he would describe that floating sensation. He was fully aware that, first Gertrude, then Mr. Spencer, had held him, carried him in their arms like a mewling baby, but he remembered the sensation as being like the out-of- body experience people often recount in near death events, a sensation of "otherness," of his nerve endings responding to a realm somehow parallel to normal sensory experience.

In clergy workshops Andy and his colleagues were often asked to describe a moment early in life that might provide clues to the origin of their vocation.

Andy never had to search. That was the moment. No matter how often he recounted it, it always stirred a place in him beyond the reach of reason.

"Gertrude was fleshy, visceral evidence of God. At that moment she *was* God," he'd say. "She called Mr. Spencer because she thought he had the superior credential for bearing that terrible new knowledge that embedded in my consciousness that afternoon. For years I had no idea what I might do to acknowledge it, or if I even wanted to. But I always knew nothing else would ever ignite my passionate energy, for good and for ill, the way that afternoon did.

The guts and terror, the steamy, steadfast love, the sense of being exempted from gravity, suspended in an other-worldly ether, was an experience from which I never recovered. My life since, when it has been intentional, has been directed toward fulfilling the obligation, if obligation is the right word, I understood that afternoon laid on me."

~

Among therapists early age trauma has become a default explanation for influencing the direction a long, complex life might take. Many times Andy revisited the afternoon of Birdie's death, and Max revisited his rescue from Los Baños. Both never failed to describe the sensation of being exempted from gravity somehow. Neither doubted that while they experienced countless other traumas in their long lives, those moments set true north on both their life compasses.

~~~

VI

Manila, Philippines 1953

Andy and Max first knew each other as seventh-graders at the American School in Pasay City, a suburb of Manila. Andy's family had moved to Manila from New York when Procter & Gamble made an offer to his father similar to the one the bank had made to Howard Sampson 15 years earlier. Because their last names both began with S, Andy and Max were assigned home-room seats next to each other, and quickly discovered they shared an odd, slightly off-kilter sense of humor.

"Keep your eye on Mr. Jolly," Max whispered to Andy in math class the first day of school, "Every time he turns to write something on the board he grabs his crotch. I think he's got jock itch. Or maybe crabs."

Struggling unsuccessfully to control his laughter, Andy snorted, like a pig. Mr. Jolly spun around, pointing at him.

"Maybe you'd like to tell the rest of us what you find so funny, Andy," Mr. Jolly said, giving Andy a withering look.

"Sorry, sir," Andy's voice cracked. "I was just thinking about something that happened at home last night; didn't mean to interrupt."

"You might find it worth your while to give your full attention to what's going on in math class; unless, that is, you already know all this and would like to teach the class."

"Oh, no sir. Yes sir. Sorry, sir."

Max didn't betray the slightest hint he'd had a hand in Andy's outburst. He looked straight ahead, eyes glazed over, as if waiting for this distraction to pass.

At recess Andy sought out Max.

"You set me up."

"All I did was give you a little inside info about Jolly's balls. It's not my fault you don't know how to keep from letting it show when you're not paying attention. You better learn, or you're going to end up in a lot of trouble around here."

Andy liked Max, especially his outrageous sense of humor, and shared his eagerness to expose the clay feet of everyone in authority. He didn't yet know about Max and the other kids in their school who had spent those years in Japanese prison camps. He couldn't say at first just what it was, but he was aware there was something about several of his classmates that made them seem different. Tougher, sadder, distant, cruel sense of humor, friendly enough, but cautious. Andy felt lonely for the seemingly easier, casual relationships he'd had with several friends in elementary school back in the States.

Even though Max could seem as emotionally guarded as any of them, Andy soon came to consider him his best friend. They lived close to each other and their Filipino drivers alternated driving them to and from school. They often spent afternoons together at one or the other's house.

Gradually, one tiny incident at a time, Max off handedly offered Andy glimpses of his years in captivity. The first came when they were shooting baskets in Andy's driveway. Andy noticed the scar on Max's leg. Though the scar was eight years old, Max's red hair and fair, pink skin made it a deeper red than the surrounding skin. It had a smooth surface, like a burn.

"You're looking at that scar on my leg, aren't you?"

"Not really," Andy stammered, "it's just…"

"Don't worry about it," Max said. But his voice made Andy think maybe he should, "It's just something I got when we were in Los Baños."

"Oh yeah?" Andy responded, eager to hear about Los Baños, which he had overheard his parents talk about. But he sensed he shouldn't seem too anxious to ask about it.

"That's where the Japs took us after Santo Tomas."

Max seemed to assume Andy understood what that meant. And maybe it was all he was about to reveal. Max slapped the basketball in his left palm, faked left, pivoted right and launched a hook shot over his head. It banked off the backboard and swished through the net without touching the rim.

"You gotta do it with your left hand. If you miss you're P-I-G."

"Not fair," Andy protested, "you're left handed; I can't shoot a hook shot with my left hand."

"Fair?" Max responded sarcastically, "You're expecting things to be fair? You better stick to playing with little kids and girls. Now shoot or admit defeat. And you have to do it from the exact same spot."

Andy switched the ball into his left hand, making a clumsy effort to toss it over his head toward the basket. It went straight up in the air, nearly hitting him on the head as it came down.

"Good try," Max said, "you make a great pig."

In the first half of their seventh-grade year Max and Andy's friendship expanded to include Pat. They became a regular threesome. Max and Pat had known each other since third grade when Pat's family returned to the Philippines from the States. Pat's father had been a guerrilla fighter against the Japanese occupiers until after liberation—miraculously and heroically evading capture while smuggling food to the starving prisoners in Santo Tomas and Los Baños. He had sent Pat and his mother and brother back to the states six months before the Japanese invasion.

Max and Andy both liked Pat. He shared their anti-authority humor and wasn't a part of the swaggering in-group who stopped by the Chinese convenience store next to school most afternoons to buy Old Gold cigarettes and San Miguel beer. At the end of the war Pat's father had "liberated" a PT Boat from the American Navy. He had converted it to a speedy, spacious pleasure craft. As Pat's friends, Andy and Max spent many a weekend and longer holidays on the Floretta, cruising the Philippine waters and putting in at remote harbors dotting the island archipelago, some of which had seen precious few white westerners.

One hot night after supper, the Floretta anchored in the harbor at Iloilo on the Island of Panay. The three boys decided they wanted to take a swim. Pat's father—the boys called him Uncle Jock—laughed when they asked him if it was OK.

"Sure, go right ahead. Of course we'll have to shine a light on the water so we can keep track of you. And to retrieve what's left of your bodies after the sharks—that will be attracted to the light—have finished with you."

"That's not true, Uncle Jock," Max protested. "You're just trying to scare us."

"Think so?" Uncle Jock asked. Then, turning to his captain, "John, shine the spot on the water."

Suddenly the water was churning with an abundance of creatures roiling the surface. Another moment and the first fin moved stealthily alongside the boat. The water erupted violently as the shark snapped its huge mouth around a school of smaller fish.

Uncle Jock laughed. Pat, Max and Andy stared down at the carnage.

"But, don't worry, those sharks aren't much interested in boy flesh, Uncle Jock said, "so if you want to swim, feel free."

What to believe?

Without a word, Max stepped over the railing and jumped into the water, making a cannonball splash.

"Jesus!" Andy exclaimed, "What the..." Uncle Jock and John roared laughter. And Pat jumped in.

Torn between his fear of being eaten by a shark, and his fear of being considered a coward, Andy hesitated—long enough, he hoped, to see if the sharks would attack his friends—and then, in a moment, the memory of which could stir an adrenaline rush in him the rest of his life, drew his deepest breath and leaped overboard.

It would be another 50 years before Andy would again knowingly swim with sharks. In San Diego he swam among the harmless leopard sharks that kept tourists out of the water. But when he jumped into the water that night in Iloilo he hadn't known the sharks in the harbor were also harmless to humans.

Nor had Max. And Max had jumped first.

The tension among their threesome and the other mostly American and European kids they hung out with, and the group of rougher boys—Mestizos, a couple of Chinese, several Filipinos—grew intense as puberty loomed. Girls became of more urgent interest, channeling the boys' energies into primordial biological longings and territorial conflict.

Their racial and national differences exaggerated their natural adolescence stresses. Andy was new to this mix of racial and national diversity. He didn't get it that Mary Jane, who could make him behave like an idiot, was a mix of American, Spanish and Filipina. All this despite her Anglo name.

Or that the Mestizo and Filipino boys considered her off-limits to the American boys. Andy invented excuses to talk to her and Mary Jane did nothing to discourage his attention. Max warned Andy: "Pinky and his guys are pissed at you about Mary Jane."

"All I'm doing is just talking to her."

"And all I'm doing is just warning you."

One afternoon after school, Andy, Pat and Max were getting Cokes at the Chinese tienda across the street from the school. As Andy stepped off the porch of the store, he was surrounded by several boys from the rival group. Pinky, the enforcer who always led them into combat, stepped out from the group and positioned himself a foot in front of Andy, his clenched fists by his side.

"We're sick and tired of you trying to put the make on Mary Jane," Pinky snarled.

"I'm not putting the make on her." The Coke bottle felt heavy in Andy's hand.

"Bullshit!" Without further warning Pinky punched Andy in the face, knocking him over backwards. The Coke bottle shattered as he fell to the ground. Pinky was on him like a wild animal, pinning his arms to the ground with his knees as he swung his fists into Andy's face and body.

Trying to turn his face from side to side to evade the stinging blows, Andy was unaware of Pinky's friends shouting encouragement.

He didn't see Max grab Pinky by the hair, yank him backwards off Andy and spin him around until they were face to face. Max had a five inch Balisong in his hand, the Filipino version of a switchblade. He pressed the blade against Pinky's throat drawing tiny beads of blood. Andy would remember later thinking that Max was nearly a head shorter than

Pinky, and that it was hard to tell whether the expression on Pinky's face was more surprise or fear.

"Keep your fucking hands off him or this knife slits your fucking throat."

"Whoa, cut it out! What's going on here, what's this all about?" Mr. Jolly waded into the middle, and the group parted. Andy saw Max slip the Balisong into his pocket. Mr. Jolly looked down at Andy on the ground, his nose blooded, his eyes already beginning to swell. Andy began to sob.

"Pinky," Mr. Jolly shouted, "you're coming with me to the headmaster's office. Now!" For a moment Pinky looked as if he was going to protest, maybe even resist, then shrugged his shoulders and followed Mr. Jolly back across the street and through the front gate of the school. Mr. Jolly looked back over his shoulder. "The rest of you, disperse; get out of here, go home. Andy, get yourself cleaned up." He took Pinky by the elbow and led him inside.

All the boys began walking off in different directions. "Let's go," Max said, as he leaned down and offered Andy a hand. Andy sniffled, his breath involuntary hiccoughs as he struggled to keep from bursting again into hysterical crying.

"You're OK," Max reassured him. "Asshole didn't even pack a strong enough punch to break your nose." When they were out of earshot of the others, Max said, "For God's sake don't cry. I don't care how much it hurts, you just can't cry." Andy drew a deep breath and began breathing more normally. He wiped the blood and snot from his nose with his sleeve.

"The next time you get into something like this," Max went on, "don't wait for the other guy to make the first move.

As soon as you're sure there's no way out of the fight, you swing first, hit the other guy in the face as hard as you can.

"It all happened so fast I bet you didn't even realize that before Pinky pinned you down, you got in a pretty good lick on him. Really surprised him. I don't think he had any idea you packed such a punch. I actually think he was sort of relieved when I pulled him off you. He was afraid if you got loose he was going to have to face a tougher guy than he expected."

Andy didn't remember hitting Pinky. Had he, or was Max trying to make him feel better, not such a coward? Whichever, it made Andy grateful for having Max for a friend.

Max brushed dirt and gravel off Andy's shoulder, a seemingly offhand gesture that to Andy was anything but. He had never felt closer to anyone in his whole life. Despite Max's instructions about how better to manage the next fight, Andy made a silent pact with himself never again to get himself into anything like this.

"Thanks for what you did back there, Max, he really had me in a shit spot. You saved my ass."

"Your ass wasn't really on the line with that jerk. That's what friends do for each other. You'll probably have to do it for me some day."

Andy's eyes were beginning to sting. He had a cut on his cheek that felt like he'd had a tooth pulled. He didn't reply to Max's saying he'd have to do the same for him. He hoped not. He didn't carry a Balisong and he didn't think he'd have the balls to challenge Pinky.

~~~

VII

Salisbury School

Toward the middle of their eight-grade year, Max's father and Andy's father had a conversation about their sons' futures at the American School.

"I don't know about you, Howard," Charlie Coffer said, "but I am increasingly uneasy about these boys spending their high school years in Manila. They're pretty adventuresome kids and there are just too many dangerous adventures for American boys in Manila."

"I share your concern, Charlie, but I'm not sure what the alternative might be. I intend to spend at least the next 10 years, if not the rest of my career with the bank here. There's Brent School in Baguio, but I'd like Max to be able to have enough experience in the States so he can decide if that's where he wants to live."

Part of the arrangement for ex-pats working for American companies in the Philippines was company-paid tuition at an American boarding school, and one round trip a year during their high school years. Andy's father had gone to Salisbury, a boy's boarding school in the hills of western Connecticut. But Max's father knew nothing about American boarding schools.

Charlie Coffer's days at Salisbury were among his happiest memories. His nostalgia and loyalty to the school made him dream of sending Andy there since the day he was born. He remained in close touch with the school through his brother who had also gone there and returned after college and the Navy to teach Spanish at the small rural school. Charlie sent a sizable annual contribution, both from his love of the school, and in hopes it might gain Andy favorable treatment should he apply.

When Andy's father wrote his brother that he hoped that Andy might go, and perhaps his friend Max, too, his brother wrote back by return mail saying the school would be pleased to have a couple of boys from the Philippines.

So it was arranged that Max and Andy would travel together on a Pan American Clipper, a four-engine behemoth nearing the end of its tenure in the last decade of commercial prop plane travel. The flight was a series of 10-hour legs, from Manila, to Guam, to Wake Island, to Honolulu, to Los Angeles to New York, 50 hours in the air. Being old, the Clipper often had engine problems along the way, which meant that Max and Andy shared adventures that would have been hair-raising for most, but were welcome sport to two teenage boys.

Looking out the porthole on the starboard side of the plane just over five hours after leaving Guam for Wake, Andy saw smoke and flames coming from the outboard engine. Before he could call Max's attention to it, the engine feathered and stopped. As other passengers became aware of something amiss, the pilot came on the intercom. In his military-trained monotone he announced, "Folks you may have noticed I've feathered engine number one. She was running rough, making handling inefficient, so we'll just fly without her. These buggies are made to fly with three—or even two—engines, so the only difference will be we'll drop down to a little lower altitude and lose a few minutes' time. No need to be alarmed."

Andy appreciated the reassurance, though he knew enough to understand that was the pilot's job even if he was bullshitting, which Max assured Andy he was.

"He didn't mention that he feathered the engine because it caught fire. Yeah, he can fly the plane on three engines, but it means he'll have to hang onto the stick for the next four hours, and it will feel like a bucking bronco."

As always Andy was impressed at Max's sophisticated knowledge of seemingly endless things of which Andy felt woefully ignorant. But he was only partially reassured.

A half hour later another engine, on the port side, smoke, fire, feathered, stopped.

"Folks," the captain's voice, still droning, expressionless monotone, "we're just snake-bit today. She'll still fly fine on two engines, but we're going to take her down to 1,000 feet. You may be able to spot a shark or two from there. But we won't charge you extra for the tour. Just relax—drinks are on the house until we hit Wake—and since the air strip is only a couple feet above sea level, you can consider we've already made our approach. We may bump around a little at that altitude but we'll do fine.

"Meantime, why not practice putting on the life vests that are under your seats. We're wearing them up here and they're surprisingly comfortable. You can take them home as souvenirs."

Andy's heart thumped in his chest. As the plane descended he began to see features—whitecaps, odd shadows in the water he'd never seen before.

"Holy shit."

As they put on the awkward, uncomfortable life vests, Max laughed. "Boeing built this baby to stay up even if a couple of its engines get shot out. Course that assumes the other two will keep going. Enjoy the view."

Andy never knew if Max was as carefree and comfortable with danger as he seemed, or just enjoyed teasing and torturing Andy. Despite Max's attempts to teach Andy to curb his fear after the fight with Pinky, Andy never mastered the discipline of keeping an untroubled façade in the face of something scary.

They limped along without further incident, landing on Wake as the pilot had predicted, requiring only that the landing gear be lowered. As the engines reversed and the plane coasted to a safe stop, they were surrounded by emergency equipment. The passengers joined in a rousing cheer, enthusiastic as their fatigued and alcohol-sodden brains could muster.

It wouldn't be the last time the two of them would spend a night on Guam or Wake to wait for repairs or a new engine to be flown in from Tokyo. They were housed in the officers' quarters which, while the older passengers grumbled about the Spartan accommodations, suited Max and Andy just fine. Though still in their teens they had the run of the place, including unlimited bar privileges, as if they were commissioned officers.

One year, put up at the Imperial Hotel in Tokyo by Pan Am while a different plane was flown in, Andy invited the stewardess, an exotic Chinese-Portuguese beauty from Macao, to go to dinner and the movies with him. Max gave him a sly, knowing grin as Andy left their hotel room for his date.

"Whatever you do," Max counseled, "don't let her know how old you are. That would completely wreck any chance you have with her."

Andy hoped Max couldn't detect how nervous he was. He always hung back from their schoolmates' chatter about their conquests, never knowing how much to believe, not wanting to expose his own inexperience. He just listened, hoping to pick up tips without betraying his ignorance. Max didn't join in either—except to crack the outrageous, salacious jokes for which he would become renowned at Salisbury—but he seemed so worldly and sure of himself that Andy figured he probably knew his way around the bedroom as well as he seemed to everywhere. Max never bragged. Andy assumed it was because he didn't need to.

"Those who talk don't do, and those who do don't talk," Max said.

Irene Matos made Andy's heart flutter when he met her in the lobby. She looked beautiful in her stewardess uniform on the plane. Dressed up for their date, she was show-stopping gorgeous.

"Don't you look handsome," she said as Andy walked into the lobby. She took his arm. Andy felt light-headed. Irene had suggested an Italian restaurant and an American western movie starring John Wayne. Andy was grateful she took the lead in deciding what they would do; he would have been stumped.

The food was good and the movie tolerable, though the theater seats were built for Japanese-size people and Andy's long legs, already cramped from hours on the plane, began to ache. A half hour into the movie Andy unintentionally brushed Irene's hand with his. She opened her palm and closed her fingers around his hand, sending a rush of blood to his nether region. The rest of the movie was a blur for him as he struggled to form a plan for what might lie ahead.

In the taxi on the way back to the hotel Irene said, "I'm weary, Andy, and I have an early flight tomorrow; I hope you don't mind if we just go back to the hotel."

"No, of course not," Andy responded, unsure if he was being invited to her room, and if so, whether he would know what to do when they got there. "I'd thought we might have a drink in the bar, unless you're too tired."

Irene smiled sweetly. "Andy, how old are you?"

Max's counsel flashed through Andy's mind as he calculated how much he thought he could credibly add to his sixteen years. "Nineteen," he said, hoping the involuntary squeak in his voice didn't give him away.

"Andy, I'm 26. I think you are the sweetest, handsomest boy imaginable, but you're three years younger than my little brother. It's been a wonderful evening; I've had such a fun time. I hope you understand that I need to go to my room now and get a good night's sleep."

She leaned across and kissed him gently on the lips. Andy's penis felt as if it might burst his zipper. He was a confusion of stirred up and relieved, his body primed for what might have come next, and the rest of him grateful not to have to figure out how to manage it.

When they arrived at the hotel Irene wrote her name and address on the back of an envelope and handed it to him.

"Write me, Andy, I'd love to know what you are up to. And thank you for a perfectly wonderful evening." She gave him a warm hug (*did she feel my hard-on?*), turned and walked to the elevator.

Andy watched her until the elevator doors closed, his emotions in a turmoil. He pushed the button for his own elevator and returned to his room.

"Nice evening?" Max asked, as Andy opened the door.

"Perfect," Andy answered, hoping his answer was sufficiently ambiguous. He was grateful Max wasn't the sort to push him for details.

"You're one lucky guy," Max said, "She's a beautiful girl."

~~~

VIII

Boarding School

Except for a hellish hard time adjusting to rural, western Connecticut winter, Max flourished in the hardy life of a boy's boarding school. The school was modeled after English public schools, designed to harden recruits for serving the far reaches of the empire. Max understood that Britain's empire days were in eclipse, a legacy now settled on the United States. He savored a chance to bond with boys who would be tapped to manage the American empire. He wanted to be ready when he would be charged with what he considered his share of the burden.

The culture didn't suit Andy as well.

Their two years in that rigorous, high Episcopal, all-boys boarding school played a major role in fashioning the seemingly opposite trajectories each of their lives would take.

They were roommates just for that term. The school thought they would be too strange, coming from the Philippines, for boys from New England to live with. One morning they slept through the rising bell, arriving late to dining hall for breakfast.

The penalty for being late to breakfast was a mile run. It left little time to eat before they had to show up for morning duties, then daily assembly, in which they were called out for being late to breakfast and publicly given demerits for doing their morning jobs unsatisfactorily.

As they were running in weather at least 20 degrees colder than the coldest day in the Philippines, dressed in mandatory sport coat and necktie, Andy began to complain bitterly about the rigid rules, the nasty weather, the sadistic upperclassmen, the total lack of pleasure in life at the school.

Max responded, "Hey, I think this is pretty good fun. I love matching wits with these guys who think just because they're a couple of years older and have more privileges and power than we do, that they have us by the short hairs."

"Well they *do* have us by the short hairs," Andy said. "They hold all the cards in this game and we won't have any cards worth playing for at least a couple more years."

Despite being short of breath and beginning to limp on his bad leg, Max made his high-pitched, sarcastic laugh, his trademark response when something struck him as pathetic. It was a mark for which colleagues would admire him, and enemies hate him.

"You don't know shit about how real power works, do you Andy? Those asshole seniors act the way they do around us because they're scared."

"Yeah? Scared of *what*?"

"Scared of *you*, Jerko. They know their so-called power is based totally on the way this place is set up. Has nothing to do with whether they're really that tough. They understand that the day we get out for Thanksgiving vacation in just a couple of weeks, everything that gives them the upper hand right now disappears into thin air. So they're hoping they can intimidate you enough now, that you would never dare challenge them when they don't have all this bullshit to fall back on.

"The way you make it work for you is to give them all that power for these dinky little things like running a mile when you're late for breakfast. Then, when the tables are turned you lay in wait for your chances."

Andy envied Max's sense of how to exploit power. It made Andy wary of him. He knew Max understood how little prepared Andy was to play power games. He never doubted—and had occasion to witness—Max's radar that could detect any sign of weakness. Andy inevitably fell for the upper classmen's bluster. He'd surrender the upper hand, as he had in the fight with Pinky at the American School. He was grateful for Max's loyalty. It felt like protection. Despite watching Max often cynically shifting loyalties among their classmates as the power flowed in different directions, Andy came to trust that Max's friendship and commitment to him weren't fleeting.

The friends' time at the school ended after their sophomore year, when Max's father wanted him to come back to the Philippines and help with his ailing mother. Andy also left then, in his case because of his hatred of the sadistic

Lord-Of-The-Flies existence. He went on to a smaller, gentler boarding school on the Rhode Island coast.

He missed Max, but didn't feel the need for his shelter as he had at Salisbury.

Neither gave much thought at the time to when or whether they would see each other again. Though they each went on to college in the States, Andy's family moved back to the U.S. The two boys' lives each went its own way. Each had a fascinating, complex life career. Neither formed another friendship as close as they had those four years as adolescents.

~~~

IX

Fifty Years Later

Contact

From: **andy@gmail.com**
To: **maxman@comcast.net**
Subject: This really you?

If this is really you, Max, this is really me, Andy. Even after all these years, I still feel like you're about the best friend I ever had. Of course we were kids then and God knows how a half century may have changed us? I'm not much interested in going back to the reunion, but I'm pretty interested in reconnecting with you. You have my email now, so if that interests you, let me know.

From: **maxman@comcast.net**
To: **andy@gmail.com**
Subject: Oh yeah, Andy!

First of all, what's with this Rev thing, Andy? You get born again? If someone asked me how I would describe the guy who was my best friend growing up, the first word that would come to me might be irreverent. If it doesn't offend your piety to spend time with a crusty old spy, I'd love to reconnect.

From: **andy@gmail.com**
To: **maxman@comcast.net**
Subject: You shitting me?

Irreverent feels like a badge of honor, especially coming from my old friend. Spy? Really? For them or for us? Or maybe one of those corporate spies, who steal trade secrets. I remember you as smart as hell, and afraid of nothing, so I bet you're the real item. I retired after 30 years as a parish priest. Four Parishes, first three roughly the northeast, last one in southern California. Living now in rural Vermont, except winter, when we take a place in California. Married to Alice, we have a daughter, no grandchildren yet. Fairly good health, pretty active for an old guy. Love to have a face to face.

From: **maxman@comcast.net**
To: **andy@gmail.com**
Subject: You come here

CIA type spy. Google me. Had the shit beaten out of me one night in Tehran, so am no longer on the travel roster. Living in a remote spot, high up in the Blue Ridge mountains outside Charlottesville. We got a lot of catching up. I'm having as much trouble picturing you as a priest as you may have picturing me as a spy. You better come here. And soon; I doubt I'm going to be around a lot longer. I'm not much for talking on the phone, but my number: 434-728-3926.

~

From: **andy@gmail.com**
To: **maxman@comcast.net**
Subject: Ready or not

I've made my ticket non-refundable so I hope you don't change your mind. Maybe crazy, but I'm not passing up a chance before I die to actually remake maybe the only real friend I ever had.

From: **maxman@comcast.net**
To: **andy@gmail.com**
Subject: Bring it on!

I was pretty sure I didn't give a damn about having friends any more. Doesn't rank high on spies' wish list. But you and wife Sandra—was CIA too—convinced me it's worth a try. When you get your rental car and put the directions in the direction gizmo, it may give you the runaround. Just get to the little store in our town, park there and call. Sandra will come down and drive you up to our place. It's a purposely treacherous drive. Not for rookies.

"Purposely treacherous," Andy said to Alice, "that sounds ominous."

"Didn't you tell me both Max and Sandra were CIA? Alice asked. I don't think I'd expect them to have a welcome mat at their front door. Being inaccessible must become a habit after a while in that world. Maybe being a spy turns a person into a recluse, sort of like being a priest can."

"Yeah, but for pretty different reasons," Andy protested.

"I wonder if they're as different as you like to think?" Alice said.

~~~

X

In The Flesh

The following Tuesday Andy took a flight to Charlottesville, rented a car, drove 45 minutes through beautiful country dotted with horse farms and pulled into the parking lot of a funky little country store. Not certain he was in the right place, he went inside and asked the woman at the cash register if she knew Max Hartman.

"That the guy who lives up on the mountain? Yeah, I know him. Nice guy. Still alive? Seen his wife, but not him for a long time. Looked pretty bad last time I saw him."

Andy bought a Dr. Pepper, went outside and dialed Max's number.

"Hey Andy," Max recognized Andy's number. "Sandra will head down to pick you up. Takes about 20 minutes."

While he waited, Andy took out his phone and flipped through the emails he and Max had exchanged. The Wi-Fi signal was weak and spotty. Andy had time to think about what he was getting into as he re-read the emails.

This has to be among the weirdest things you've taken on. It's not as if you're lonely, or don't have enough to do. What's in it for you to probe a friendship from 50 years ago that your memory has no doubt made into something it wasn't? You're a sucker for intrigue and power; maybe this is another of your voyeur things. You know how well those worked out in the past. Yeah, yeah, all true enough. But none of the old pieties I mouthed all those years do it for me any more. Max was my best friend as a kid, and Alice is right that I haven't made real friends since I became a cautious, ordained adult. So what's so great about friends? OK, dipshit, keep on kidding yourself that you don't need friends. I bet that Jeep is Sandra. In for a penny, in for a pound.

Sandra jumped out of the wreck of a Jeep, stuck out her hand, and when Andy grasped it, pulled him into a bear hug. "I can't tell you how much Max has been looking forward to your visit. And me just as much."

Andy pushed the lock button on his rental and with the habitual grunt his leaning over produced, slipped into the passenger seat of Sandra's car.

"No more than I have," Andy said. "It's a little unnerving how our friendship has come back to me as vividly as if we'd never lost touch."

Andy thought Sandra might have winced when he said that. As they drove up the treacherous, winding road she probed Andy about what he was expecting in this meeting with his old friend.

"I don't know what you remember of Max," she said, "but he's been pretty beaten up over the years. Every bit of the fire you may remember is still burning in him, but his body is fragile now. A lot of people think he's depressed. He's not."

Andy took that in without commenting. *What does Max remember of me?*

After a 20-minute ride that seemed to Andy like a terrifying obstacle course, Sandra navigated the Jeep onto a narrow gravel path between two huge trees and down a final steep descent into a scooped out place in front of three narrow steps leading to a wood bridge across a gully, Sandra stopped, motioned toward the massive front door and announced: "Home again, home again, jiggidy-jig."

The door swung open. Max stood in the doorway, leaning on a cane, wearing a wide grin. "Welcome, old friend," he said in a hoarse, gravelly voice. "It's been a long time."

My God, do I look that old to him? Andy wondered.

Andy got out of the car and took the steps and bridge with as much of a sprint as he could manage, conscious of wanting to seem spry. At the door the two men reached for a handshake that turned into a bear hug.

"Holy shit!" Max exclaimed, "I can't believe it."

"You got the shit part right, but the holy part may be a stretch," Andy said, as they released their embrace. Still holding each other by the elbows, they examined each other's face with undisguised curiosity.

"Quick as ever," Max said, "and apparently no more pious."

"Why don't you invite him in," Sandra suggested. Max pulled Andy inside. As he came through the door Andy looked across the room to the far side, all glass, a 100-mile view of the Blue Ridge Mountains.

"Some spot you've got," he said. "Don't imagine you have a lot of big dinner parties. Your guests would never make it back down that road alive."

"A spy's career doesn't make for a big social life," Max explained, "not, so I'd imagine, like yours."

"Lots of social life as a parish priest," Andy answered, "but turns out to be more part of the job than about close friends."

The three of them were still standing just inside the door. Sandra and Andy had on heavy coats and muddy boots.

"OK, you two," she said, "you've already discovered you've got enough to talk about. How about we give Andy a chance to freshen up and then we can have some of that fried chicken I made this morning."

An aging priest and an aging spy, sniffing each other out like hounds from the same litter, long separated. Fifty years since, without really having to work at it, they renewed a closer friendship than either had formed since.

~~~

XI

Max, the spy, believes—hopes—he has spent his life nobly protecting his fellow citizens from evil people and nations that would otherwise do them harm. Some of what he has done causes him to fear for his immortal soul. That's hardly a metaphor with Max. He believes in a god who keeps score, and while he thinks his scorecard has some stars for heroics, he's not sure they outweigh the black marks for things he did while he was protecting his fellow citizens.

Andy, the priest, led anti-war groups, preached against American imperialism, wrote op-eds about the foolishness of American hegemony, preached sermons contrasting American power with Jesus' teaching about humility. He's never believed in the immortal soul, nor in the god Max thinks keeps score. He has been nagged by a sense that the safe pulpit from which he has preached God's universal love, and against military force as a strategy for peace, was made possible by the danger people like Max have faced down.

Neither yet senses that they will look to the other for absolution. Max, for reassurance that the evil he has done is justified by his motives and the results. Andy, for reassurance that his preaching of peace was motivated more by integrity than the draft exemption his ordained status provided.

~

They walked into the den that led into a long, recently added room beyond. Andy was taken aback. Guns, weapons of every sort, on the walls, the floor, in bookcases, filled the rooms.

"Surprised, huh?" Max said.

Max and a handy man had built an addition to his house on the isolated mountaintop in rural Virginia, doubling the size of the original house. The addition accommodated is prize, the world's largest collection of assault weapons in private hands.

"There's a weapon here from every war our country has ever fought," Max explained, "including the revolutionary war. From both sides in the Civil War."

Andy, tried to disguise his unease. He surveyed the array of weapons surrounding him. His attention was riveted by a submachine gun on the floor, its clip of brass bullets seemingly in place for firing. He decided not to ask Max if those shells were dummies.

Max seemed amused by Andy's discomfort.

"I never understood the stock market." Max said, "I invested in something I understand better—weapons. I know a lot about weapons. The world eventually tires of horses and cars, TVs and computers, but it will never tire of new toys for killing each other. These weapons are what I think are called liquid assets. I can turn them around for a profit tomorrow."

After a few minutes of conversation, some reminiscing, some cautious references to what had commanded their interest over that 50 year period, Sandra invited them to come to the dining room. When they were seated Andy and Max were at opposite sides of a small oval table. Sandra was at the end closest to the kitchen.

It immediately became clear that neither man had come to this meeting for small talk. They were risking unfamiliar territory, friendship they remembered from long ago but hadn't tested with anyone since. Max waded in with what had been on his mind since he first discovered Andy through email.

"I'd be fascinated," Max said as the three of them sat down to Sandra's fried chicken, "to know where you were and what you were doing in the fall of 1983. I ask because I think that's when I think I earned my bucks the most. When we may have come closest—even closer than the Cuban missile deal—to actually trading nukes with the Soviets. I've always wondered how much people really ever knew about that. And how people who didn't know were spending that time. Even more than some of the more seemingly dicey stuff I got into. When I'm feeling the need to justify how I spent my life, those few days in 1983 have always seemed to me the strongest argument for spies I can come up with. There was stuff that might make for sexier scenes in novels, but none where the stakes were higher."

Andy sensed he was being tested. Max seemed to be probing for whether Andy was going to judge his life as a spy. He had to admit he was squeamish about whatever Max was about to tell him. Andy was also fascinated. And he was eager to explain to Max what had led him to his own life path.

"Even in my most pacifist phase," Andy said, "I don't think I questioned the need for spies. I'd be eager to hear what went on then. I've always suspected those of us who were chanting, 'All we are saying is give peace a chance,' were pretty unaware of what you were facing."

Max smiled, relieved, grateful that his old, new friend seemed open to maybe challenging some of his own history.

"It began with a massive NATO war game, practicing for a possible nuclear war. Reagan had pronounced the Soviet Union an evil empire and Andropov, who became the Soviet leader after having run the KGB, was gravely ill, creating a vacuum in Soviet leadership. All that led the Soviets to believe the US was about to use the Soviet's chaotic transition moment to launch a surprise nuclear first strike.

"I was riding a desk at Langley headquarters. I hated the desk jobs that regular rotation required, but I was a man under authority, following orders.

"So I found myself at what turned out to be ground zero in the nearest nuclear confrontation between USA and the Soviets since the Cuban business.

"Able Archer was the name assigned to the NATO war game, simulating a nuclear exchange. I was assigned the job of assessing how successful we could be in preparing a first strike on short notice if we detected the Soviets intended to go first.

"I wasn't privy to the operational details of our plan but I was given intelligence—mostly obtained from the Soviet double agent Oleg Gordievsky—and ordered to assemble a report on how much the Soviets knew about Able Archer, and how they might respond.

"Everything I saw led me to think the Soviets believed our war game was cover for a planned first strike by us, not a practice exercise. I thought long and hard about how to deliver that opinion to Bill Casey, our then-Director, who was a Wall Street lawyer. It was well known that he was easily excited. But my assignment was to decipher the intelligence, not judge the Director's mental state. The information seemed too solid and too critical not to pass on."

"Holy shit, Max," Andy said. "you had to tell Casey you thought the Soviets misunderstood our intentions, and you feared Casey was trigger happy? Did you consider softening the language in your report that in some way would weaken what the intelligence suggested? You must have wanted to keep him from overreacting."

Max bristled. "Something you anti-war birds never understand is the way command works. Once you sign on for the job I had, you don't get to decide whether to pull the nuclear trigger. That's way above your pay grade. You may think the Director, or the President, is an asshole who can't think straight, but you either honor the command structure, carry out his orders or resign."

"I didn't mean to suggest you should have withheld information, Max. But when does your personal judgment have a higher calling than your orders, especially if you think mistaken judgment by the person you're reporting to could result in mutual annihilation?"

"Never," Max said. Andy sensed the prickliness his question had aroused in Max.

"So maybe you'll answer a question for me, Andy, about what you peacenik priests were doing while we were scrambling planes and people so, if it was inevitable we could get our nukes over their targets before theirs could get to ours?"

"Praying," Andy answered without hesitation.

"Well done," Max said, with less sarcasm than Andy would have expected. "Thank God your prayers were answered."

"No need to make light of me, Max," Andy said, hearing the defensiveness in his own voice. "Of course we were organizing demonstrations, writing telegrams, making phone calls to our representatives."

"Well I can tell you," Max insisted, "your demonstrations and phone calls had zero impact on Casey or Reagan. It must have been your prayers."

"I don't want to mislead you, Max. I didn't mean to suggest that I think prayer can actually change events like that."

"Didn't you, Andy? Don't you believe it can? Or are you another of those frustrated do-gooders who went into ministry because it gave you a platform to carry out your political agenda? Not because you were a believer?"

~~~

XII

The conversation had taken an uncomfortable turn Andy hadn't seen coming. Max's question was one Andy had asked himself over and over. And he never came up with an answer that let him off the hook. He was chronically uneasy about letting his uncertainties show. He knew people sometimes considered him an agnostic. *Maybe I am.* In all those years he'd never figured out just what he believed about prayer. And now Max was challenging him pretty belligerently.

"Is that a serious question?" Andy asked. "Are you asking me if I think prayer can alter atoms and molecules, change outcomes?"

"You're fucking right it's a serious question," Max said. His intensity unnerved Andy. "I spent my career collecting information, turning guys on the other side into our agents, even killing a couple of people, all the time telling myself what I was doing—some of which went against what I had always believed was right—was justified. Sordid as it sometimes was, I believed it might prevent either our country being overrun by our enemies, or the world ending in nuclear conflagration. That, and a modest amount of patriotism, are the reasons I did what I did. But there are still moments that could make me hate myself if they can't be justified by the result.

"And if you want to know the honest-to-God truth—pardon the pun—I always hoped there were some sincere sky pilots like you, praying your asses off. Because there were plenty of times when I doubted our efforts were going to be enough to help us get through the crisis."

For an uncomfortably long time the only sound in the room was the scraping of spoons against bowls as the three of them finished their dessert.

"And you want to know something more, Andy?" Max finally broke the silence. "I prayed my own ass off the whole time. I prayed not only that what I was doing would help prevent what scared the daylights out of all of us, but also that my immortal soul might be spared, even though I was lying and killing, committing mortal sin.

"I hoped guys like you, with turned around collars, your knees calloused from praying, knew something about the big guy upstairs that I didn't. I hoped your prayers could keep from happening what I was scared shitless all our hard work couldn't.

"Did I think your prayers were really that powerful? I fucking depended on it, Andy. And you want to know something else? I still do. So for Christ's sweet sake don't tell me you think it's a crock of shit."

For Andy, this exchange was as unnerving as 50 years ago when the Board of Examining Chaplains had asked him about his prayer life before they were deciding whether to recommend him for ordination.

He'd been warned about that question by a couple of friends who had gone through the process a few years earlier. They'd coached him on how to fudge his answer so he didn't lie exactly, but didn't sound like the fraud he always worried he was.

The issue of prayer—what it is, how it works, if it works, whether he had a disciplined prayer life—had nagged Andy through 30 years as parish priest. He'd gotten as clever, or so he thought, at satisfying dying people, divorcing couples, parents of terminally ill children, as he had the examining chaplains.

But this was different. This was Max, his old, new friend, asking sincerely, almost desperately. Was he going to evade the question again, now, retired and more than 70 years old? To what end?

"You know, Max, I'm not sure I can tell you exactly what I know you want to hear."

Andy began to explain, stuttering awkwardly. Max cut him off: "So you're not really a believer. You're an atheist. Well done." Max's sarcasm was thick. "You should have been a spy, Andy. Pretending to be someone you're not is lesson number-one for spies."

"Hang on," Andy objected, "I didn't say I'm not a believer, or I don't pray. Or that I don't think prayer matters. It's just that the idea of God's mind being changed by my prayers—I find it awkward to even speak of God's mind—doesn't square with the ways I think about God. Which I have to admit, even after all this time, is a lot less clear than I wish. Do I think that God hears my prayer and decides to turn Andropov's mind? That God puts it into his head that the U.S. was only practicing, not about to launch a strike. I have to admit I don't. That's why we depend on you spies. Do I think prayer matters? I think it's as essential as breathing, and just as mysterious and beyond reach of consciousness."

"Well if that's too big a stretch," Max bit off another question, "what exactly is the point of prayer? I understood the point of what I did, some of which turned my stomach, was to protect my country. And I hoped, prevent the world from destroying itself in nuclear war. What exactly was the point of what you did?"

As he said that, it was as if the air had suddenly been let out of Max. Deflated, spent. Andy, too, felt spent, defeated.

Maybe this was a big mistake, thinking our childhood friendship could bridge the vast distance between what we've done with our lives.

"I apologize, Andy," Max said, his voice subdued, gentle. "That was uncalled for. I really didn't mean to attack you. Or put you on the spot. I'm sure you're a sincere guy. With integrity. It's just that sometimes I'm haunted by things I did in my job. And I can't stop hoping someone—someone like you I'm afraid—will help me believe it was OK."

"Believe it or not, Max, I'm pretty much the same," Andy admitted. "Maybe for a lot of the same reasons. I never thought of myself as a liar, but I sure as hell skated cautiously around some pretty hairy moments, when people looked to me for reassurance about things that felt way above my pay grade.

"I can't pretend to understand what prayer is, how it works, if it does. I'm not sure I even know how to pray. Or if there is a right and a wrong way. Or how to help someone else pray. I pray, I think, in ways that I believe are real. I mean, my emotional and mental energy gets powerfully focused on things that I think matter. And, I'm sorry to say, often on things that probably don't. We clergy like to let ourselves off the hook by saying that prayer is about changing the one doing the praying, not the things being prayed for."

Andy was aware that Max and Sandra were both listening intently, reading his expression.

"I believe that. I know it begs the question we all want to know. Is prayer a form of energy that makes things happen? Do I think praying can actually influence physical events.

"To me, that's sort of like asking why women and men have sex. Yes, we hope to make babies—except when we don't. *Enough with the cleverness, Andy.* And yes, we know about sperm and eggs. But mostly, I think we do sex the way all animals do, with scary primordial energy we don't understand.

"Well yes, sex is how we reproduce, but we both know sexual energy comes visiting even when it's an inconvenient time to make a baby."

Max laughed. "For Christ's sake, Andy, do you clergy birds ever just do shit, have a spontaneous moment without having to diagram and decipher what every atom in you is up to? I believe in prayer, pray just about every day, but can't say I ever prayed before I got laid."

They all laughed. "Oh hell yes, Max, don't I know. But we always hope we don't wreck our lives because of having given in to our impulses. God knows, clergy have as strong impulses as anyone. And we all heard stories of their impulses bringing them down."

"Now that's where your job and mine came pretty close," Max said. "To survive, a spy not only has to do good spying, but learn to discipline his impulses. Giving in to impulse in the spy world leads to disaster."

Andy hesitated several moments before responding. "I'll have to think about that some, Max. I'm not sure we're talking about the same kind of impulsiveness."

"Remember hearing about that Ambassador who was shot by terrorists?" Max asked Andy. He didn't wait for an answer. "I was the last CIA guy left with him in the embassy, along with a couple of Marines. It was my job to keep him safe." Max's eyes filled. He pulled a Zippo lighter from his pocket, flipped up the lid with that old familiar metal click and tried to light a cigarette. His trembling hand was unable to hold the flame still long enough to find the tip of the Marlboro dangling from his lip.

Andy was stunned. Spellbound. After a long silence, he regained his voice.

"Ever read about that bishop in Ohio who ended up shooting himself after it was revealed he was having multiple affairs with women on his staff?" Andy asked Max. "I locked horns with that guy over accusations by a guy in my parish who accused me of encouraging him and his wife to get a divorce. I think that bishop wanted to depose me for malfeasance in office. It doesn't exactly rise to the level of your horror story about that ambassador, but it went on for a couple of years and made me wonder if my life as a parish priest was over."

"Did you encourage them to get divorced?'" Max asked.

"Well, in a way, yes. And no. No, because I wasn't stupid or arrogant enough to think I could make a decision like that for anyone. Yes, because they weren't stupid, and they knew I thought their marriage was a snake pit that was poisoning both of their lives. It was one of many times I felt like I was in over my head. In fact the guy may have quoted me accurately when he told the bishop I lost my cool in one of our counseling sessions and said, 'If you two aren't going to work any harder than this, you may as well get divorced.'"

"Did anyone die because of it?"

"No, at least not literally."

Max's hand finally steadied enough for him to light his cigarette. He inhaled and laughed at the same time, choking, coughing. Andy, though he was concerned at Max's distress, sighed with relief at his laughter.

"Jesus Christ," Max said, when he finally caught his breath, "and I don't use that name lightly. You and I have some catching up to do.

"I've been pretty consistent in telling people who ask that it was my intention to serve the country that rescued me as a little boy," Max said. "But I'm almost old enough now to own up to a bunch of other less noble motives. I'm addicted to adrenaline. Not so much personal danger, though if that is part of the package I'll buy it."

"Yeah, I like excitement, too," Andy said, "but I'm basically chicken when it comes to physical danger. The kind of excitement that attracts me is what goes on inside people, the stuff we'll normally do everything in our power to hide.

"I preached a sermon once, still young and naïve, in which I said, 'If you could fly over this town like Superman, and like Superman, use your X-ray vision to look through the roofs of people's houses, you'd be amazed at what people are struggling with.'"

"What they heard was, 'I am Superman, and I have flown over your house and seen what you're struggling with.' The next day my phone rang off the hook with people asking to come see me.

"They figured now that I knew their secrets they may as well come talk to me about them. And come and talk they did.

"I told my wife I wished I'd never preached that sermon. The truth is I never felt more useful."

Sandra had thoughtfully left them to talk in private. After an hour's conversation Max and Andy owned up to a common thread in what motivated them. And that much about that motivation wasn't as noble as they and their admirers like to think. The conversation was intense from the get-go. And it shook them both. Neither had ever before been so candid, maybe not even with themselves.

"When that GI picked me up and ran me out of the Jap camp where I had been at the mercy of those pricks for nearly four years, the thrill was in knowing he was stronger than the Japs who had treated me like their plaything. And he was an American. Like me. I don't buy all that chauvinistic hype about being part of the most powerful nation on earth, but it sure made being a spy for our country more fun than I think it must be being a spy for some half-assed country."

After some silence, Andy gave his version.

"A large part of me hates that Christianity has run the western world for the past two millennia. That kind of power corrupts priests, bishops and popes just the way it does everyone. I'm not so cynical that I'd say the church has been a malevolent force, but whenever it's gained great power it's done great harm.

"But I confess I didn't object to being given a piece of the prize that went along with it. The moment I put on that turned around collar people treated me differently. I can't think of another line of work that would so instantly have won me the respect and access that did. And I hadn't done a thing to earn it.

"I'm not proud of how much I liked that, and I hope I've mostly kept from abusing it, but I certainly accepted it without protest, even though it often grated on whatever conscience I have."

~~~

XII

As they were finishing lunch, Max turned to Andy and asked, "How're you with guns?"

When Andy first saw Max's collection, he'd wondered when this would come.

"Not so good," Andy admitted. "Except for BB guns, shooting at tin cans as a kid, and one skeet shooting session with an almost, but not quite father-in-law, I've never fired a gun. Dad was phobic, wouldn't have one in our house. I'm pretty phobic myself."

"I've got a treat for you, Andy. I've got the handgun that saved my life, and cost the two guys who jumped me in Tehran theirs. I've got it in a drawer in my study. Something makes me think you'll understand a little better what those 50 years have made me if you were to fire that gun, like I did. That gun's the only reason I'm sitting here talking to you instead of pushing up daisies. What say?"

"With all due respect, think I'll take a pass," Andy said.

"Look, Andy," Max's voice turned hard. "I don't think you understand what this is about for me. You're a guest in my house, my oldest friend. You and I are exploring how those years when we never saw each other shaped us. You're willing to know me, not abstractly, but from the inside? You need to fire that gun."

"Gives me the willies," Andy admitted.

"All the more reason you need to do it."

Andy's armpits became damp. He never trusted himself with any sort of weapon. Years of therapy convinced him he lacked good impulse control. He'd learned to discipline himself, back away from situations in which his impulsiveness could cause great harm. The maybe three times he'd fired a gun it aroused a fantasy in him that came closest to what he imagined schizophrenia might be like, disembodied voices commanding something destructive he would never ordinarily consider.

What if I turned this gun on that guy pulling the clay pigeons?

"I really respect what you're saying, Max, but I don't think it's a good idea. I've got this weird thing in me about guns."

Max was resolute, beyond reasoning. "Your firing that gun has everything to do with your understanding this guy you called your best friend all those years ago. Hate to seem hard-ass, but we're talking deal breaker."

Andy relented. "OK."

Max rose from his chair, a lighted cigarette hanging from his lip, walked into the study, pulled open a drawer and lifted out a handsome wood case.

"This is the only reason I'm alive," Max said, as he unlatched the box and took out the handgun. "That night in Tehran, those two guys who jumped me beat me almost to death. One of them stuck a Kalishnikov in my face as I lay on the ground, screaming 'CIA!,CIA!' They were better armed than I was but I was better trained. I managed to get my hand on my service revolver and shoot them both before they could shoot me.

"Probably tells you how fucked up my head still is about all that, that I need so badly for you to fire this."

Andy felt light headed.

Max put two bullets in the chamber and locked the safety. "Let's go out on the deck where there's nothing for miles that matters if you hit it."

Despite the cool fog Andy broke a sweat. They could see through thin ground fog across the valley to other hilltops several miles distant.

Do I really want to be Max's blood brother? What the fuck am I getting myself into?

Max took off the safety and handed the gun to Andy. It was heavier than Andy expected; his hand drooped with the weight.

"Hold it up, Andy, you don't want to shoot off a toe."

Andy managed a feeble laugh in response to Max's robust guffaw.

"See that rock out there? Try to hit it. It's close enough so you don't have to allow for gravity to affect the trajectory. Just hold the gun with both hands, like this." Max stood behind Andy, holding his hands over Andy's. When Max stepped away Andy felt abandoned. "Sight down the barrel and squeeze the trigger gently. I've put .22 ammo in there; it won't have much kick."

Andy tried to follow Max's directions, but his hand trembled, making it impossible for him to keep the sight lined up with the rock. The trigger was more sensitive than he expected, and before he intended the gun fired with a loud retort. Dirt kicked up 10 feet in front of and off to one side of the rock.

"You spared the rock!" Max shouted. "You really are a compassionate priest!"

Humiliated, Andy fired again. This time the bullet winged a tree 30 feet beyond the rock.

"Shit," he said, secretly relieved to have fired both rounds safely. Or giving way to some weird impulse.

"Hey, not bad for a rookie." Max seemed exhilarated. "At least you fired, even in the right direction. You know how many soldiers actually fire their weapon in combat? About 10 percent. You're not alone in finding guns intimidating. Those assholes that tried to kill me in Tehran would have wished I'd been among that 10 percent."

"Well, I'm sure glad it was you and not me," Andy said, a flood of relief washing over him. He had to fight back the urge to cry. *Jesus, that's what you need now, to cry. Back to the fight with Pinky.*

Andy handed the gun back to Max. They stood staring off into the distance, neither speaking. Max slid open the glass door and led Andy inside. In what looked to Andy like a practiced ritual, Max placed the gun carefully back into the velvet lined box, closed and latched the top, then carried it into the study.

"How about a cup of tea?" Sandra called out from the kitchen? "You two warriors need a break."

"Perfect," Andy replied. He sat in the Eames chair he knew Max usually sat in, but had insisted it be Andy's perch for the visit. Max came back into the room. He stood looking down at Andy.

"Can we talk about that, Andy? About what was up with you that you nearly came unglued rather than fire the gun?"

"Maybe, Max, if I can be brave and honest enough to come clean about it. Maybe it would help if you could say something about how come it was such a come-to-Jesus issue for you that I fire it."

"I thought you were going to stand down for a while," Sandra said as she came into the room carrying a wicker tray holding two tea cups and a plate of ginger cookies.

Andy laughed. "I guess we could use a referee, Sandra. When Max and I were kids in Manila we used to invent games that went on for days. Our parents would sometimes call a halt when it got too intense. Of course we were teenagers. You always think you'll become more easy going in old age."

"Guess not," Sandra said, "but maybe you could take a break, talk about football or something, like normal guys."

"Normal's something I don't think anyone has ever called me," Andy said. "Not that there's not part of me that would love to be normal. If there is any such thing."

"If you were I wouldn't give a shit about having you for my best friend," Max said. "I sure wouldn't have pushed so hard about firing that pistol with some normal guy."

"Feels great to have you call me your best friend," Andy said. "Even though I am gun phobic and I'm sure we're likely dancing around a few elephants camped out in the living room. Unless that bazooka has them scared off."

"OK, big boys, I surrender my referee job," Sandra said. "You two may as well go at it."

~~~

XIII

Secrets

And so it began. Two old men whose lives had taken radical-ly different courses, at their chance reunion, 50 years since they'd last seen each other.

"You know," Max said, "I'm glad I didn't know how you filled those 50 years. I doubt I would have wanted to check out our old friendship. Too many differences."

"Well," Andy responded, "I sure as hell would have wanted to write you off. You still seem eerily like the Max I remember from when we were kids. I guess I can square that kid with the guy who spied and lied, and holy shit, killed. Have to admit it means rearranging a lot of what I once thought were unbreakable rules.

"But, you know over the centuries reality has made the church change most of the old rules. Never admit it, but even Mother Church gets blown off her course by the changing cultural winds. A lot of those shifts are probably what made it possible for me to be a part of the Church. But when it has worked against people who are in the weakest position—slavery comes to mind—it has undermined her authenticity."

Each man harbored secrets he told no one. Each suspected there were people who knew those secrets. In both worlds, spy and priest, they had rivals, people who resented and envied them, lay in wait for the moment when they could use their secrets to bring them down. For some of the same reasons, and some different, neither ever totally let down his guard even long after retirement.

Power may not have been the driving motive for either, but in different ways each became a powerful figure. Convention may say that a spy is motivated by patriotism and a priest by faith. These two men were self-aware enough to know their motives were mixed. They learned to negotiate around rivals within their own organizations, and in the world beyond, always wary of anyone they suspected had a stake in bringing down what they believed they were working for.

Andy sometimes thought the skills required of a parish priest resemble those required of a Mafia Don.

As Andy was driven up that nearly impassible road, he'd considered the ways he, too, chose to make himself inaccessible. Inaccessible to colleagues envious of the seemingly plum parishes in which he worked. And, as Alice sometimes accused him when he vetoed people she thought might turn out to be friends, he made himself—and Alice—inaccessible to some who legitimately wanted a relationship with a priest. Some just liked them, wanted to be friends. Andy knew his suspicions had made their life unnecessarily lonely.

Spy training and clergy training each put a premium on learning to keep one's counsel. It had steeled them in self-discipline, in resisting the temptation to display their power by titillating others with hints of the inner confidences that go with the job.

It was a sign of the unusual trust they almost immediately felt for each other that as they sat over coffee at the table after lunch the conversation went to that dynamic of secrecy and its isolation.

"You know, Andy, a spy not only has to keep secrets, but he has to be willing to lie when someone is trying to pry them loose. Not so hard when you know a rival spy is working you over. But it can be really hard keeping to yourself scandalous shit you've learned about people in high leadership positions to whom you report. Especially when you have low regard for those people and their judgment. And would like to see it become public."

"Check, check and check," Andy said. "Alice discovered a parishioner we were entertaining in our house sneaking upstairs to look in the bathroom medicine cabinet. If I was taking any medications I didn't want known I would hide it in my shoes. That made us cautious about friendships.

"I finally got it that the role means people come and tell you all sorts of crazy stuff they'd never tell anyone else. You see them at their most vulnerable. You stand alongside their dead and dying. They tell you their sexual peccadilloes.

It's like you've been in their underwear drawer, seen their sex toys, what they look like naked. It can make them feel uncomfortable looking you in the eye. Often they want you gone after that."

Max laughed. "Spies wear armored underwear."

"One of the weirdest," Andy said, "was a mafia guy who came to my office and wanted to confess. I explained that while Episcopal priests do hear confessions, I suspected he had me mixed up with a Roman Catholic priest. Turns out, no, he knew what he was doing when he came to me. He wasn't about to go to a Roman Catholic priest who was liable to be tight with other mafia.

"'What I want to know,'" the guy asked me, "'is if you're bound by the seal of the confessional.' I told him I was, but if something he told me seemed to put someone else in danger, I might seriously consider breaking confidence.

"You know what that sucker did? He reached into his pocket and pulled out a pistol and put it on my desk.

"'Now you're going to have to think about whether you're going to break confidence,' he said. He told me about having killed a couple of rival gang members."

"No wonder you're phobic about guns," Max laughed. "They should have issued you a service revolver when you were ordained."

"What I found startling," Andy continued, "was I realized he was more scared of going to hell than getting caught. He figured his chances of being killed, soon, were pretty good. And he was looking for absolution that would at least get him out of hell and into purgatory."

"Holy shit," Max said, "your job was almost as much fun as mine. I understand that guy's anxiety about going to hell better than I wish. What did you do?"

Andy laughed. "Funny now, but it didn't seem funny at the time. I told him I thought God's love could overpower anything in the universe and that if he repented, was sincerely sorry, maybe God could forgive him. But I told him I didn't have the authority to grant absolution. Since there's no way he could make restitution. He couldn't restore the lives he snuffed out. So that was between God and him. Only God can forgive like that. I may be a priest but I'm a human priest. I'll absolve those whose penance can restore the injustice but not an irreplaceable life."

"Was that enough for him?" Max asked.

"I don't think so," Andy said, beginning to understand that for Max this was more than just an interesting story. "Because of what he said next.

"'Just so you know,' the guy said, 'if I ever thought you'd told this to anyone, I wouldn't hesitate to use this.' He rotated the gun on my desk so it pointed toward me.

"'And just so you know,' I said, 'I'll put a memo of this conversation in my safe deposit box, and tell my wife if anything happens to me she should look for a memo in there.'"

"Good work," Max said. "I'm surprised he didn't pick up the gun and finish you right there. What did he do?"

"He said, 'I forgot you fucking guys are imposters, have wives.' Picked up his gun and walked out."

"Had he been fingered, and someone knew about his having come to you, would you have revealed that conversation?" Max asked, his head enveloped in an exhale of smoke.

"I ask myself that question a lot; still not sure."

"Did you put that note in your safe deposit box? And did it make you feel safe?"

"I didn't have a safe deposit box."

"OK, cool. I rest my case, Andy. You birds were at least as good at expedient lying as we were."

~~~

XIV

How Secret?

Secrets. Only their wives, who slept with them, heard what they said in their sleep, knew. Neither Andy nor Max were ever certain how much their wives knew. They would have been startled, uneasy and grateful, that after nearly 50 years their wives knew, directly or intuitively, even the darkest secrets. Andy and Max intended to carry those secrets to their graves.

~

Andy retired Episcopal priest, rector of several large, establishment parishes, lionized by many. Max retired spy, decorated undercover CIA agent. Icons, symbols, bearing the projections of those who hope someone is managing the chaos. Aware so many consider them icons, equally aware of their own foibles, weaknesses. Neither Max nor Andy have ever wholly found peace with having carried projections they knew were weightier than reality would support.

Now they are old men, no longer distracted by ambition, their lust reduced to occasional fantasy. Cautious edginess has become an unexamined habit. As the two old men began testing unaccustomed intimacy, that calloused reticence began to soften.

Neither grieved the lack of close friends (though their wives periodically called them out on it). It surprised them to find themselves ripe even if still wary, for something, someone, to break open that part of themselves so tightly and purposefully closed so long ago.

This guy has been taught to break through people's defenses, Andy thought. *Your charm has served you well over the years but won't cut it with him. This is piss-or-get-off-the-pot time. He's too savvy for you to think you can cajole him into cutting you slack.*

A priest, Max thought. *Spy training isn't exactly preparation for true confession. If you're not up for this best face it now, before you find yourself unloading a bunch of stuff you've always been so careful to keep under wraps.*

They regarded unguarded candor as a luxury for people with different lives, less explosive secrets. They were practiced at the wiles their jobs called on. They accepted and embraced disciplines that hid, even often from themselves, any lingering hunger for intimacy. Neither any longer pushed against the constraints of their jobs because they didn't consider them restraints.

To rekindle their childhood friendship now, at 71, could tear the cover off that discipline in ways neither Andy nor Max would have consciously set out to do.

~~~

XV

Max & Andy Reintroduce Themselves to Themselves

"Jesus, Max," Andy said, "I can't remember the last time I used a Zippo."

"Or, I suspect, the last time you had to endure someone blowing smoke in your face," Max said. I made a brief try at quitting a few years ago, but I'm perverse. Every form of political correctness turns me the opposite way. I figured I'd be dead by now whether I stopped smoking or not. Smoking is the last pleasurable bad habit I can still manage."

Max leaned toward Andy handing him the Zippo. It bore the CIA logo. Andy was taken aback by how familiar the lighter felt in his hand, more than 40 years since his last cigarette. He flipped open the lid, spun the tiny wheel, mesmerized by the flickering flame and puzzled by the pleasure it elicited.

His mind drifted to an experience that helped form him as a new priest.

"Early in my first job," he said, "I got very close to Andrea, a woman who was in the hospital dying of lung cancer. Tells you how long ago. She and I used to smoke in her hospital room. This was early in the days when the dangers of smoking were first being reported. Andrea would chastise me.

"'I'm an old lady, doesn't make any difference for me. But you're young (I was 27). Your whole life is ahead of you. You ought to quit.'

"I would sit for hours talking with her. I was fumbling my way toward feeling legitimate about being a priest. Spending time with her as she died helped me understand being priest in ways seminary hadn't. I don't think it had sunk into me that she was actually dying until the night my phone rang at 2 A.M. It was her daughter. Her mother wasn't expected to last the night. I mumbled something and hung up.

"'Who was that?'" Alice asked. "When I told her, she told me to be careful, driving to that part of town in the middle of the night. Until that moment I was still trying to work out how not to go. Alice made me understand I had no choice. *You're a priest, remember, asshole? You tend the dying.*

"When I got there, Andrea was unconscious, struggling for each breath. Her daughter and son-in-law were sitting in chairs at the foot of her bed. Both smoking! I took a chair next to them and lit up my unfiltered, king-sized, Pall Mall. The three of us sat there filling the air with smoke as the poor dying woman gasped for breath. Her daughter and son-in-law kept looking at me expectantly until I got it. They were looking for me to do something priestly. I stood up by the side of the bed, took Andrea's hand that wasn't plugged into an IV, began mumbling a prayer, trying to remember words. I had forgotten my Prayer Book and would have felt awkward reading something rather than speaking spontaneously. It was such an intimate moment.

"Suddenly Andrea opened her eyes wide, yanked my hand with surprising strength, raised herself off the bed. 'Oh no, not yet!' she exclaimed clearly with startling energy. Her eyes that had been closed were now staring a hole through me. 'Hold me!' she demanded. I froze. 'God damn you, Andy, hold me!'

"That shocked me out of my stupor. I reached around and through all the IV lines she was plugged into and put my arms around her as best I could. I have no idea how long that lasted—probably a few seconds—until, as suddenly as she had come to consciousness, Andrea lapsed back into unconsciousness and went slack in my arms. I carefully withdrew my arms, trying not to pull out any lines, went back to my chair beside her daughter who was sobbing. Her daughter's husband stared ahead blankly, zombie-like.

"I lit a cigarette.

"I suppose it was a few minutes later that the three of us became aware Andrea wasn't breathing. Her daughter went looking for the nurse, who finally came, put her stethoscope on several places on her chest, pulled back her eyelids, letting them close again, and said, 'She's gone.'

"Seemed like the nurse looked at the three of us accusingly—especially me. I projected that she was thinking that if I had done something more useful than sitting there smoking, maybe Andrea wouldn't be dead.

"Did I think that? Maybe. I damn sure didn't feel like I had done anything very helpful."

"Sweet Jesus!" Max said, "it's like the movies."

"Well, I didn't have a script and I barely managed not to wet my pants.

"Andrea's daughter's sobbing became louder. I'm not sure how much longer we stood by the bed, staring blankly at her body. I remember feeling like she might open her eyes and speak to us. I kept watching her chest for some movement. None of us spoke. I think it was the son-in-law who suggested leaving, and we did. Just as we reached the door it suddenly occurred to me that I should say a prayer. I turned around, went back to the bed, stumbled through what I could remember of the Aaronic blessing (unto God's gracious mercy and protection we commit you...), screwed up my courage enough to touch Andrea's already cooling forehead, made the sign of the cross. Dead, for sure."

"As the proverbial doornail," Max said, expelling a lungful of smoke.

"Dawn had just begun to color the sky as I crossed the parking lot to my car. As I approached the car I pulled a cigarette out of the package in my shirt pocket, reached into my pants pocket for my Zippo—no fancy logo—and, about to light up, said out loud, 'You dumb shit.' I took the cigarette out of my mouth, crumpled it and the package in my hand and threw it into a wire trash basket in the parking lot.

"That was my last cigarette, more than 40 years ago. I kept my Zippo for many years after that. I finally gave it to the thrift."

Max seemed moved by Andy's story. He thought about it in silence for a few moments, then broke into laughter.

"Hate to think of you wasting a perfectly good pack of Pall Malls. I wonder, was she the first dead person you'd ever seen? Seems like it scared the shit out of you."

"Yes, except for my grandfather, all made up in a coffin. What seemed really weird was when the nurse said she was actually dead, it seemed kind of unexpected, a shock. Dead? She didn't look much different from how she'd been two minutes earlier. Is that what dead looks like? Too fucking subtle. I was exhausted from the night's vigil, and probably from hiding how scared I was. I was in the early stages of learning how to let my turned around clerical collar run interference for me. Andrea's daughter and son-in-law probably didn't realize what a rookie I was. They must have assumed this was routine for me."

"We apprentice in spy school for years," Max said. "They wouldn't turn us loose in the big leagues until we'd proved ourselves. Seems like they let you guys play in heavy traffic pretty early."

"A couple of weeks later," Andy continued, "my boss sent me to represent him at the wake of the high school principal who had killed himself after the newspaper revealed that he'd been stealing money from the football team's utility fund. It was my first wake, confronting a corpse, all gussied up. I was meant to lead the show for the mourners. I realized I can seem calm and together when everyone else is coming apart. Soothing words come pretty easily. Once I'd memorized a couple of prayers I felt like I came across as the real thing.

"Truth was, looking down at that waxed corpse, it took every ounce of self-discipline not to faint. I still think the line between alive and dead is too vague."

Max stubbed out his cigarette and lit another.

"Every time I go in for surgery," he said, "which these past 10 years has been about as often as most people get haircuts, they have to cajole, maybe bribe some anesthesiologist to put me to sleep. Smoking and high blood pressure make me a terrible risk."

"You were the most stubborn—make that determined—person I knew when we were kids," Andy said. "But since you've been having all these medical challenges have you considered giving up smoking before it gives you up?"

Max laughed. "Nope, never."

Their 71 years began to weigh on both men's stamina. This first meeting was an emotional bath, the kind of unprotected encounter they had always avoided. It was the most unguarded conversation either had, with anyone, since they were boys back in Manila.

"I'm exhausted," Max said. "My back is good for about half as long as we've been at this. What say we call a recess? You have an early morning flight back, and I've got a morning appointment with my surgeon.

"I'm more pleased than I can say to have this time with you but I need a rest. You've got to promise you'll be back again soon. I feel like I'm on borrowed time and we've got a lot more to explore."

"I'm the same, Max. I promised Alice I would be back in one piece, which I won't be if I don't take a timeout. I'll be back, likely in a month or so. I feel like some piece of me that went missing many years ago is finding its way home."

Sandra drove Andy down the mountain. She and Andy embraced before he got into his rental car.

"How was your time?" she asked him.

"Unimaginable," Andy said. "As if Max and I had stayed in close touch all these years, even though we didn't, and had no idea what the other had been up to."

Sandra smiled. "That's a huge gift. Rare that a friendship from that long ago, especially between two people who have been up to such different things, can reconnect like that. Don't you wonder why this seems to have worked so well?"

"I do. Maybe something to do with both of us having lived lives in which so much of what mattered most had to be kept secret. Maybe that's what made us simpatico. Not that we told each other those secrets, but that we appreciate what it cost each of us to keep our counsel."

Sandra's smile gave way to a skeptical expression. "You do know, Andy, I worked for the Agency too. Even so, I've always known there were things Andy didn't tell even me. I hope you're not expecting to learn some big national security secrets."

Oh shit, Andy thought, *she's been through this before. I bet sometimes she's had to guard Max against this.*

"No, Sandra, I totally understand. My pastoral confidences will remain confidential. And I'm not looking for Max to reveal stuff and then have to kill me."

They both laughed.

"Well, no one can have too many friends in this life, sure as hell spies can't," Sandra said.

Choosing to ignore the double meaning in her comment, Andy said, "Priests sometimes make the fatal mistake of thinking people who cozy up to them want to be their friend. Most priests can only be real friends with other priests, and most of the time they are too competitive to be friends you'd trust with anything very edgy. I guess that's why it seems like such a big deal to find Max the friend I remember."

"I think it's great you two have found each other again," Sandra said. Andy wasn't convinced she really thought it was that great.

~~~

XVI

Andy's Dream

On the flight home Andy fell asleep on takeoff and woke just as the plane touched down at Bradley Field in Hartford. He dreamed that Max came to his church, though he wasn't sure which one, and held a forum following the service, which was billed as "Things You Never Knew About Your Rector."

In the dream Andy squirmed as he sat at the back of the parish hall behind parishioners who seemed delighted to hear whatever titillating things his old friend might reveal. It frustrated Andy that when he woke, the dream was still vivid and made him anxious. He couldn't recall any of what Max had actually revealed, only that it embarrassed him and seemed to titillate the parishioners.

What could he have told them that would make me squirm? Neither of us revealed anything really scandalous about ourselves. But after 50 years, two-thirds of them as parish priest and spy, there sure as hell have to be more than a few skeletons in both our closets.

Years of therapy and mindfulness had taught Andy a dream like that was an invitation to fill in some blanks. *Maybe they're blank for good reason?*

Meeting Max again, feeling so connected, was pretty unexpected. Feels like one of those rare chances to unpack dicey stuff in a safe place. But that's a little crazy, considering a relationship with a spy a safe space. Isn't that why you've kept going with a shrink all these years? Having a safe place should you ever actually want to spill the beans?

Andy was grateful to get home, feel familiar ground under his feet. Cosmos, their Norfolk terrier, jumped up on him with his usual enthusiastic greeting. Andy's curiosity about the secrets Max was revealing in his dream, faded.

~~~

XVII

Reset

Alice was in the back field harvesting tomatoes when she heard the car drive in. She came in the back door, dew rag around her forehead, her pants torn and mud stained. Andy found the sight of her hugely reassuring. Their embrace wasn't the perfunctory embrace with which they usually greeted each other. Andy clung to her. Alice finally took a step back, looking at Andy quizzically.

"How was your trip? What's Max like now? Hot down there? Plane crowded? Any problem getting your bag? You must be hungry? When was the last time you had anything decent to eat? You must be tired. I've been out harvesting; got plenty for tonight's dinner."

Andy didn't try to respond to Alice's barrage of questions. It was her habitual way of reconnecting.

She gave him a quick kiss on her way to the sink where she began washing vegetables.

"Been really hot here," she said. "Must have been hot there, too." She turned and opened the cabinet beneath the stove, taking out a colander, rinsing the tomatoes. "How's Sandra? I bet she's got her hands full with Max having so many health issues. And I bet he misses all the spy intrigue. Do they still have that dog they love so much? And what about his weapon collection? Weren't they going to begin giving that to a museum?"

Before Alice paused for a breath, or Andy could assimilate her questions and comments, she was gone, off to the pantry to find a vase for the flowers she'd picked from her perennial garden.

When she came back into the kitchen, Andy came up behind her as she stood at the sink, put his arms around her, kissed her on the back of her head.

"It was a great visit," he said, "and I missed you."

"Would you go out to the kitchen garden and pick me some chives?" Alice asked, "and then maybe you'd make some cream cheese and chive dip for hors d'oeuvres for tonight. It's a perfect night to sit on the porch and watch for the beavers to come down to our end of the pond.

"I think I'll make some pesto and put it over pasta for supper, if that appeals to you."

"Love it," Andy said, though Alice was gone again, too soon to hear him, this time to check a pesto recipe online in her office.

~~~

XVIII

Retired Spies

When Sandra arrived back from dropping Andy she came into the den where Max and Andy had been meeting. Max was in the Eames chair, feet up on the footrest, fast asleep, snoring.

Max woke a half hour later. Sandra said, "Had a nice good bye with Andy; sounds like you two hit it off famously."

"Way better than I could have expected," Max said. "I felt more relaxed and willing to be straight with him than I can remember with just about anyone. He's the same good guy from when we were kids."

Sandra stood in front of Max, giving him a long look. "Best be on your guard," she warned. "He's a seductive guy. You may be retired, but you've still got plenty of secrets that need to stay secret. Once a spy always a spy."

"You know, Sandra, I sense he's got a slew of his own secrets."

"Yeah, he hinted at that when we were saying good bye. Just be careful. It's so comforting to feel like you've got someone with whom you can let go of that caution you've had to use all those years. There is no such person, not even Andy."

~

Max's nightly Ambien worked better that night than most nights. He slept soundly from 10 to 1:30, got up, peed and fell back into uninterrupted sleep until nearly 7, the longest uninterrupted sleep he could remember in years.

No nightmares in which he saw his KGB agent being tortured and executed.

"I kept checking to make sure you were breathing," Sandra said when he appeared in the kitchen where she was cooking sausage. "I don't think I've ever known you to sleep more than three hours without waking up."

Max smiled. His hair was disheveled from sleep. He shuffled in his lamb skin slippers. His old woolen bathrobe was held by a frayed sash.

"And what would you have done if I wasn't breathing?"

"Call the new Director and tell him he could take you off his list of loose canons he has to worry about," she said without hesitation.

"Whoa, that came out pretty easily. You must have been thinking about that a lot."

"No, no more than I used to about Aldrich Ames."

"Jesus, Sandra, what's this bug you've got up your ass? Someone at the agency ask you to keep an eye on me?"

"No, sweetheart, sorry. Sometimes all that stuff that got drilled into us in training can come very close to paranoia. It's your visit with Andy. I could tell from the way you two greeted each other and the energy that was flying around the room as you talked, that it was like a religious moment for both of you. And the way Andy hugged me when he left. He mentioned what it meant to be able to talk with someone the way you two talked to each other…"

"And what about it?" Max asked, his sleepiness giving way to full attention.

"I don't know. Maybe I'm jealous. One of the things I knew I was giving up when I signed on with the Agency was being able to have the kind of friends you long for as a kid. Since I never really had friends like that even as a kid, it didn't seem like such a big deal at the time.

"But seeing the way you and Andy were, I guess I was a little jealous.

"But not only jealous. Also wary. I'm sure I don't have to remind you about how we learned in training that everyone, even the most independent and disciplined of us can be seduced by seemingly warm, unconditional friendship. And how there really is no such thing as unconditional friendship; always a quid pro quo of some sort."

"You think Andy's a counter spy?"

"I don't think anything, Max. I'm just using the skills we learned, and chief among them is having your antenna up for signals, especially for unusual warmth since everyone on earth, including the toughest spy, is hungry for that."

Max felt a wave of exhaustion, as if the brief encounter with Sandra had wiped out his good night's sleep, and his unusual euphoria after his time with Andy.

"That sausage smells great," he said. "How about I go brush my teeth, comb the few hairs I have left, put on some clothes, and we have breakfast out on the terrace? From the forecast I think this may be the last morning we'll want to do that for a while."

"Lovely idea," Sandra said. She put her arms around him and kissed him firmly on the mouth. They held their embrace for several moments.

"That ups my appetite for more than just breakfast," Max said.

"You're more easily seduced than I ever imagined. No wonder they retired you. Well, breakfast is about the most you can expect from this old bag this morning. If you'll set the table on the terrace I'll finish cooking."

Max went into the bathroom. As he brushed his teeth he addressed his wrinkled reflection in the mirror. "No one said it would be simple."

~~~

XIX

Alice and Andy Meet the Elephant in the Living Room

Several hundred miles and many states to the north, Andy and Alice were eating oatmeal laced with raisins, walnuts, brown sugar and yogurt. They sat at their round kitchen table overlooking the 20 acre pond.

"Seen the otters recently?" Andy asked.

"Saw them once while you were away," she answered. "Not sure, but I think there may have been a little one with the parents."

"Oh wouldn't that be sweet," Andy said. "I hadn't seen them for a while. I'd worried they might have left."

"Surely you've learned a new dimension of patience," she said, "what with having rediscovered your oldest friend after all these years."

"You know, Alice, that's a pretty apt analogy. Not that I'd thought much about Max during those 50 years, but if I had I would certainly have assumed I'd never see him again. And that if I did, he would seem like a stranger, not like the brother I always wished I had and he came close to being back then."

"Very sweet, Andy. Amazing that you two clicked like that.

"I suppose your conversation must have come around to Rick Ames at some point. That must have been weird."

Andy's heart skipped a beat.

"No, in fact it never came up."

"You're kidding. Your once, maybe next longest standing friend after Max, the most notorious traitor in CIA history, and you didn't say anything about it to Max?"

"No. Should I?"

"Gosh Andy, I would have thought so. You and Max have more in common than those years at the American School in Manila and Salisbury. But Max doesn't know that. Yet. When are you planning to tell him?"

"It never occurred to me, honestly. I mean, I know the CIA isn't a huge organization, but why should I think Max and Rick Ames had anything to do with each other?"

"Oh Andy, dear Andy, you accuse me of being naïve. Of course they knew each other. You clergy are a funny bunch. I guess it's because everyone who might be a friend gets weird about the priest thing. When you run into someone who might be a legitimate friend, you're so eager for it to work you turn a blind eye to anything that might kill the deal?"

"That stung," Andy admitted. "It just didn't come up."

Alice put her hand on Andy's neck, massaging gently. "Look, Andy, of course it's your deal. I know how much this means to you. If it were me and I thought it might be the real thing, I think I'd find some way to mention to Max that we had been friends with Rick. When he discovers you had a close relationship with Rick—remember, he's a spy, he'll find out—it might kill the deal. If he thought you'd purposely avoided it, or been too much a coward to own up to it, don't you think he'd be pissed? Or worse?"

"Maybe even suspect something more sinister, being a spy after all."

That stung.

"I'll think about it."

After breakfast Alice went off to run errands. Andy went to his writing studio over the barn intending to work on a couple of poems he'd promised his editor he'd have ready soon. He sat at his desk staring into the blank computer screen, not bringing up the poems.

Who do you think you're kidding? Rick Ames was your senior warden, tennis partner, your daughter's godfather, your confidant. Max's entire professional life was turning and protecting foreign agents. And you think Rick Ames, who's famously known to have caused the execution of at least eight CIA contacts in the KGB, didn't have a major impact on Max's life?

~~~

XX

The Uncovering

From: **andy@gmail.com**
To: **maxman@comcast.net**
Subject: That great visit

Hey Max, that time with you was mighty powerful. Incredible that the closeness and affection we enjoyed as kids seemed every bit as real 50 years later. I am so looking forward to our next visit. There's something about finding you again that's like reconnecting a missing link in my life.

BTW, I probably should have mentioned that Aldrich Ames (yes, that Aldrich Ames) was a close friend before he went off the rails. I had known him when he was a parishioner at my parish in D.C. He and I became tennis partners, played in a few tournaments. He is godfather to our daughter. I was as shocked as anyone when he was caught. I knew his weaknesses, a little grandiose, womanizer, had a tendency to live beyond his means, but never imagined it would lead to anything like it did. I can imagine how you guys in the Agency feel about him, and of course I share your feelings.

Anyway, water over the dam, long time ago. And, I hope, doesn't diminish the strength of that friendship we renewed.

Best to you, dear guy, and thanks to Sandra for letting me hog a day of your life.

Hope we can schedule another visit before too long.

Andy

Andy hesitated before hitting Send.

Maybe it doesn't matter. That was a long time ago. Rick has been in prison so long it's old news. He's not the only old friend I no longer have anything to do with. He and Max probably had nothing to do with each other. Get real, Andy. If this matters to Max, and how could it not, keeping it from him will have an effect like an affair does in a marriage. Now maybe that's a little over the top, don't you think? I mean, yes, it was a great reconnecting so powerfully with Max but it's not as if you were getting married. OK, Andy, enough. If it wasn't really an issue you wouldn't have begun the email in the first place.

He hit Send.

~~~

XXII

What?!

"Sandra," Max shouted from three rooms away, "you're not going to fucking believe this."

Sandra came into Max's study. She was dressed in her yoga sweats.

"Sitting at your computer, shouting at me as if you were having a heart attack is hardly kosher, Max. You know I don't appreciate that. What's so important that it couldn't wait until I finished my yoga workout?"

"Sorry, Babe, but you gotta' read this."

Max got up from his chair, motioning for her to sit. She did, silently for a minute.

"Well, I'll be god damned. What are the odds?"

"Of all people, fucking Rick Ames. How could Andy have been a friend of that asshole?"

"Well, Max, at least for a brief time you thought Rick was OK. He was a colleague, even a friend, after all."

"Bullshit! I thought he was an unreliable piece of shit when he interned at the Agency while he was in college and I couldn't believe it when they actually hired him. Much less when they put him in that job that gave him access to all the KGB stuff my agents were feeding us. Jesus, Andy's judgment sure sucks."

Sandra got up from the chair. She stood looking at Max, then took his face in her hands, looking in his eyes. She smiled.

"Max," she said, her voice quiet, gentle, "is it that your feelings are hurt, or are you wanting to write off your old/new friend as an accomplice of Rick Ames and the KGB?"

"I don't know what I want right now, Sandra. I just know I wish I never had to hear that prick's name again. I can taste that old anger as if it all just happened."

"How are you going to respond to Andy's email?"

Maybe I just won't." Max's jaw stiffened.

"Oh, you've got to, Max. But I think it would be good if you waited a while. Let it roll around in you. I mean maybe it'll be a deal breaker between you two, but I bet not. I figured there'd be some sticking points between you but I'd never have guessed this one. But it's not as if you had friends to spare. On the off chance Andy might yet turn out to be for real, maybe you don't want to blow him off while you're so upset."

Max was silent, looking at Sandra as if he was expecting more.

"You were the one who cautioned me not to let my enthusiasm at finding an old friend make me let down the guard we spies promise to keep up for life," he reminded her.

"And my caution stands," Sandra said. "Andy's a priest, a bleeding heart. Just the kind of person a shit like Ames could con. That doesn't mean he can't still be your friend. Just don't let his unusual openness and warmth seduce you into forgetting your hard-learned disciplines.

"Even though you've been retired for a long time, I shouldn't have to remind you, Max, that there are still people out there, especially a few of those guys in Tehran and Baghdad, who would love to even the score with you. I don't put Andy in that bunch by any stretch of imagination. But you just never know how some indiscretion on your part could escalate into a long ago, never forgotten jihad.

"But look, don't fly off the handle and diss him too fast. Andy's a priest. He knows about screwy relationships, even if he may have been fooled by Ames. I don't think you need to blow him off yet."

Max sat on that email for several days, considering whether to email any response, or whether to send a blistering rebuke. His anger having softened over time he sat down to respond.

From: **maxman@comcast.net**
To: **andy@gmail.com**
Subject: Ames

Have to admit, Andy, that knocked me back! This isn't a suitable medium for unpacking all that brings up for me. Maybe we could plan a meeting on some neutral ground soon. I have a friend who has a house he hardly ever uses on an island off Virginia. He has said he'd be happy to have me use it as a retreat anytime. Not the easiest place to get to, eight miles into the ocean, but it's remote and quiet, a place where we could talk uninterrupted for a couple of days. I think the subject warrants that serious a setting. You?

Andy read Max's email several times. Each time it felt heavier. *I never imagined my long ago friendship with Rick would come back to haunt me all these years later. Or that I would be so eager to twist myself into knots to try to renew an old friendship from when I was a kid.*

When Alice came home he helped her with the groceries, offered to make her a cup of tea, helped put away the groceries, many in the wrong place. Alice corrected him each time until she began to wonder about him.

"What's up, Andy?" she asked. "You're preoccupied with something."

"Oh, just reading about the terrorist attacks in Paris last week. Really tests my emotional discipline not to give everything away to all the media hype."

"Well, despite your best intentions, sweetheart, you're not St. Francis. You've never claimed to be a pacifist. Give yourself a break. Everyone's in turmoil after those horrible attacks. All those young people. Terrible. And the killers were young too."

Now Andy felt worse, using the attacks to divert Alice from what was really eating at him. *But why should I have to own up every time something stirs my neuroses?*

"I got a response to my email to Max about Rick Ames."

"Oh? What'd he say?"

"Maybe you'd read it; tell me what you think."

Andy tapped the email function on his phone, scrolled to Max's message and handed the phone to Alice. She stood by the stove and read it.

"Hmm, interesting. What's your reaction?"

"I don't know. Maybe that visit with Max was a onetime thing. I can't see the point of dragging the Ames business back from the junk pile where it's been all these years."

Alice put her hand on the back of Andy's head and pulled his face toward her.

"Andy! I understand this has all brought back the shame you feel about Rick. It's embarrassing to be taken for a fool by someone you trusted the way you did him. But it looks like Max may have his own reasons to want to unpack whatever his deal with Ames is. Maybe you could both exorcise the demon that man is for the two of you. Wouldn't it be great to have a chance to set it right? Something everyone admires about you is your willingness to take a chance on someone. That you were willing to be a character witness for Rick at the trial when the whole world wanted to string him up, has always made me proud of you."

"Yeah, well that didn't work out so well did it?" Andy said, his voice whiny. We lost three of our biggest givers from the church and Rick still went to prison for the rest of his life. Serves the fucker right."

Andy hung his head. "Oh God, I talk such a good game, Alice, about facing fears, letting shame be fodder for new life. But I fucking hate thinking about what an asshole I was for considering Rick such a good friend."

"Why do you call yourself an 'asshole' Andy? Because you had a friend who turned out to have done something terrible? And who you stood up for when the rest of the world turned on him? It was Rick's betrayal and deceit, not yours. I actually think what you did, unpopular and hard as it was, was pretty honorable and brave."

"Yeah, stood up for a spy whose betrayal caused the death of a bunch of Max's guys; I was an asshole to do that."

"But you couldn't have known that at the time. I don't mean to use your own best stuff to make a point with you, Andy, but what about Judas?"

"God damn it, Alice! Judas turned in Jesus because he thought it would force Jesus' hand, make him fight back. Rick was deceitful and I was an ignorant sucker who fell for his phony pose as upstanding citizen."

"Well, of course you feel stupid now," she said, "but you've always been willing to cut people slack, even when it seems risky. And you did that with Rick. Oh, Andy, I'm not trying to be holier than thou, or smarty about this. I just hate to see you beating yourself up for being such a vulnerable loving guy."

"And I hate having you hold shit over my head that I said from the pulpit."

"Oh, Andy, sweetheart, what would it take for you to be as kind and forgiving with yourself as you were with parishioners?"

"Cut the irony, Alice. OK I admit it. Max's response got under my skin. I hate being made a fool of."

"I bet Max doesn't think you were a fool to have been Rick Ames' friend. It probably shocks him, upsets him." Alice's voice was calm, kind, not accusing. "I have no idea how Max may feel about your being Rick's friend, but I know how many people, including me, loved you urging us to be generous and forgiving even if it meant sometimes being taken advantage of. I've seen you do it again and again. And even when you got burned I loved you for erring on that risky side rather than on the side most of us choose—the much easier blaming, judging side."

"Maybe you should have been the preacher, Alice."

"What say we have a drink and watch the sun go down?" Alice suggested.

"Done," Andy agreed, exhausted. The tension had left him limp.

~~~

XXIII

Trading Emails

"Heard anything more from Andy?" Sandra asked Max a couple of days later.

"No, nothing. I wasn't expecting to because I responded to him that I didn't think email was the right forum to talk about who Ames is to each of us. I'm waiting to hear if and when we might meet again."

"What're you thinking about how you want to respond?" she asked.

"I'm all over the place. I mean, it's been years since all that. I was really happy to find Andy after all these years, but I hate to have that fucking traitor come up again and wreck another piece of my life.

"But I know I can't just ignore it. My blood pressure must have gone up 50 points when I read Andy's email. I can't pretend it doesn't matter to me."

~

"You and Max had any more emails?" Alice asked.

"Nope. Max made it pretty clear he wasn't up for exploring the issue in email. Guess we need to make another face to face time unless we're just going to drop the whole thing."

"Do you want to drop it, Andy?"

"I don't honestly know what I want. I really hate feeling like a fool, which is exactly how all this makes me feel. I don't know if I can look Max in the eye now, especially since I totally chickened out about bringing it up when we were together. Yes, I knew I should; I just hated to throw a monkey wrench into what felt like such a good thing."

"Andy, I know you're not going to throw over a chance for a real friend just to spare yourself feeling like a fool. I've heard you say too many clergy go to the grave lonely, wishing they'd been willing to make real friends. It seems like Max, because he knew you back when, and because he's such a tough bird, just might be really straight with you. And about a lot more than just Rick. What a gift to have a friend who would do that." *And maybe save me from having to do that alone.*

"I know, I know, Alice. But think about it. Max gave his whole life, his soul to that work. I feel like he might consider my having Rick as a friend and as our daughter's godfather a huge slap in his face, maybe even a betrayal of my patriotism."

"You willing to hear what I think?" Alice asked.

"Not really," Andy said petulantly, "but I bet I'm going to anyway."

"I understand why you fight me off Andy, but suppose it turns out that yours and Max's friendship is stronger than this Ames thing. One of those rare resurrection things you invite the rest of us to be alert for. Something we too rarely get to try out in real life. And you haven't even explored the Ames thing with Max to see how it plays with him. Wouldn't it be great if you not only have found your old friend, but managed to get the monkey off your back that Rick has been for so long?

"Maybe I'm over-stepping a little but I've heard you longing for the kind of friend it sounds like Max might turn out to be. He's not a parishioner, isn't all mixed up about whether you're supposed to be God. At the risk of sounding gooey religious, this might be a God-given moment in your old age."

"And if it isn't?"

"What'll you have lost? A friendship that was 50 years ago. Disappointing but pretty much leaving you as you were—a respected elder clergyman who most assume has a rich, happy life filled with significant relationships.

"Sorry if I sound like a scold, Andy, the last thing I intend. I've listened to you talk about colleagues you once thought pretty highly of, who have become boring, depressed. Maybe one reason a lot of clergy get like that is because you absorb the pastoral discipline of discretion to a fault. It's not only your parishioners who think you're supposed to be godlike. Maybe a lot of you think that about yourselves. No wonder you end up building a wall around yourselves, protecting yourselves from anyone who might actually see you're actually human, like the rest of us."

"You're being pretty relentless about this, Alice. Not like you to push so hard. What's in it for you?"

She put her hands on either side of Andy's face, a gesture she reserved for their most tender, intimate moments.

"You're what's in it for me, Andy. Maybe this would turn out to be a formal, empty gesture between two old guys still preening and posturing as if they were in the locker room after a tennis match. But sometimes I think I see better than you can how hungry you are for a real friend. When you came back from that visit I sensed something woken up in you, something I worried you'd given up on.

"And one other thing, a lot more selfish. Sometimes being the only person you let show your less noble side to can be a burden. I know you carry around things you're not proud of. If Max should be the kind of friend you don't mind seeing some of that, it would take a lot of weight off me."

Andy tried to look aloof, as if it mattered more to Alice than to him. Alice knew better than to push harder. But she was pretty sure his visit with Max had stirred in him what he liked to call a resurrection event. She'd heard him explain it that way to others who had an unexpected encounter with someone who turned out to really matter.

~

"So, Max," Sandra asked, "have you and Andy made another time to get together?"

"No."

"Are you going to?"

"I don't know. I think the ball's in Andy's court."

"Oh yeah, which of you decided that?"

"Neither, really, just seems that's the way it is. How come you're so hot for this Sandra? Last I remember you were warning me about getting seduced by an old friendship. Compromising the confidentiality disciplines we learned in the Agency."

"True enough, Max. There will never be a friendship, even with one of your old colleagues, in which that issue isn't present. But what if that fire you and Andy kindled in each other turns out to be worth feeding? Just because there are boundaries you can't cross doesn't mean you can't be friends. You two discovered each other before you were a carefully guarded spy and before Andy had a job that got him mixed up with God. If it clicked, that could be worth gold to both of you."

"I don't know, Sandra, it sounds like work. I'm retired, not looking for more work."

"You know, Max, we've talked a lot over the years about how sad it is that spies don't have friends, how they turn inward, devour themselves like a voracious tumor once they retire. We're all such masters at keeping our real selves hidden. We've both been spooked by so many of our old colleagues who have gone senile. I suspect that might be in part because they no longer have people they match wits with the way you did with each other every day when you were in the Agency.

"I like being your wife, understand better than I wish why you guard yourself. But I worked for the Agency too and I still have a couple of friends I love to spend time with because I trust them with stuff that matters to me. Not secret spy stuff. But that's not what really matters anymore, is it? What matters now is knowing a couple of people who care about how things really are with you. People who aren't just interested in what you can do for them, or what dirt they can worm out of you. And who you don't mind telling what troubles and what excites you.

"Maybe it's worth exploring whether Andy could be that kind of friend. It's not as if there are a bunch of others knocking on your door."

"But the Ames thing..."

"Max, the Rick Ames debacle is a source of shame for you, I know. Who could blame you after those agents were executed because of him? You did everything in your power to protect them. But maybe a friend like Andy, who knew Ames as a husband and father, a tennis partner, not as a spy and traitor, could open a way for you to consider all that in a different light. Maybe you could begin to ease some of the pain that shame still causes."

Sandra knew that planting a seed with Max was better than trying to muscle him into something.

~~~

XIX

Another Go

More than a month went by in which the two men exchanged neither phone calls nor emails. Andy assumed Max had written him off. Max assumed the same of Andy.

Andy finally decided to risk it. He woke several nights fretting about it. *What the hell? Why should it matter so much?* Andy, who knew a lot about himself thanks to years of sometimes painful therapy, couldn't fool himself. He knew how much it mattered.

From: **andy@gmail.com**
To: **maxman@comcast.net**
Subject: Get Together

Hi Max. I bet you considered scrapping the whole thing after our last emails. I did. Alice badgered me (I can be pretty stubborn) into seeing what a pity that might be. Not to put pressure on you with this but she's right that I don't have many (any?) friends, at least not of the kind we were as kids and I sensed we might still be. Not so much someone to whom I reveal secrets, but who gets how the strengths I've been praised for as a priest are the mirror side of the weaknesses I have always tried to keep hidden.

Now look, Max, it may turn out that we're not going to be friends like that. Though that would be disappointing, I could live with it. But on the off chance that energy I sensed when we got together turns out to have legs, I would love to take a stab at another meeting.

I'm going to propose a few days at this quirky little motel I like out in the Borrego desert, a couple of hours east of San Diego. It's remote, has a nice walk into a lovely oasis in the canyon, and the only decent restaurant in the region.

If you're willing there's a long but non-stop flight into San Diego. I could meet you and drive us out there sometime, say, shortly after the first of the year. Cold nights, sunny, warmish days.

Coyotes howl at night.

I have no doubt we have lots to talk about. Not least the weird coincidence of Rick Ames having intersected each of our lives in significant but pretty different ways. Might be too painful but it might be a way, at least for me, to unravel some of the shit I've avoided for a long time.

Let me know if you like the idea and I can make reservations.

Andy

~

"Look at this," Max said to Sandra. "I think maybe Andy just sent me a marriage proposal."

Sandra came into Max's study and looked over his shoulder at the email. She read it twice while Max leaned his head to one side waiting for her to say something.

"Max, you were maybe the best spy the Agency ever had, unbelievably discreet, but that doesn't mean you have to spend the rest of your life fending off everyone who tries to make friends. I read this email as a tentative but friendly offer to see if you and Andy might turn out to be friends. Nothing over the top, just hopeful."

"Reading it just made me feel tired," Max said. "Like I was being asked to re-enter training for the weird kinds of relationships we spent so much energy learning to navigate when we joined the Agency. I was relieved to leave that behind when I retired."

Max lit a king size unfiltered Marlboro, snapped his Zippo closed, got up from his chair, brushed by Sandra and began pacing back and forth in his study. He was careful to avoid the stockpile of weapons that dotted the walls, filled book cases and cluttered the floor. He stopped and considered the WWII machine gun mounted in the far corner, a belt of dummy ammunition fed into the magazine.

"I know what it means when you begin to pace around these weapons like a rat running his wheel in his cage."

Max turned and eyed her, arms folded. "And what does it mean, oh Sigmund?"

Ignoring his sarcasm Sandra said in a calm, matter of fact voice, "That you sense a challenge you're not sure you're up to."

"You can be so fucking smug," he accused, biting off his words. "What about that email do you think scares me?"

"Friendship," she said. "Andy must be the last, maybe only friend you had before you chose deep cover. Straight friendship's not something that's offered to any of us very often so it's no great surprise that you don't know what in the world to do with that email."

Max took a menacing step toward her. "Can you just cut this smarty-pants psycho stuff with me? I could make friends if I want. I'm not an emotional cripple. I'm a natural born spy, a loner. Truth is I don't really want or need friends."

Sandra was used to Max's hostility when she got in close. She took a step toward him and embraced him, holding him tight. Max squirmed at first, as if he wanted to get away, then relaxed, letting her pull his head into her neck.

"Oh Max, we've led a fascinating and, I believe, noble life. But it's left us with some deficits. Loneliness may be the biggest. We're not doing that weird work any longer, don't have to be so careful to never take an unguarded breath. We're not going to live forever. Maybe this is a chance to fill a big hole in whatever time's left."

Max's eyes filled, he sighed.

"I must be a huge pain in the ass to live with, Sandra."

"No, quite the opposite. Don't get me wrong about this. I love being married to you. I can't imagine anyone else who would put up with me and vice versa. But I know I'm not enough. No one person alone can ever be everything to anyone, no matter how close. I covet for you a chance for a friend like the one or two I've been lucky enough to make the past couple of years."

"But your friends weren't friends with Rick Ames."

"Oh for God's sake," Sandra said, as she angrily pushed Max away. "If it means that much for you to hang onto your loneliness... If martyrdom is what you want as your legacy, then stiff-arm Andy and anyone else who looks like a friend. But don't expect me to be able, or willing, to fill all the holes that you carry around so proudly, like battle wounds. You'll get no purple heart from me."

From: **maxman@comcast.net**
To: **andy@gmail.com**
Subject: Let's do it!

Nice offer Andy. I accept with I hope at least as much anticipation as uneasiness. I say that only to warn you that close friendship doesn't come easily for me. Thirty years as a spy didn't exactly hone that skill. But I'm retired and it seems fortuitous that my friend from longest ago should appear now. Never been to Borrego but I like the desert. It suits my preference for a minimal existence. How about we shoot for the second week in January if that works for you.

Your mostly wannabe friend.

Max

~~~

XX

"So you're going to risk it," Sandra said. "Good for you. I always knew you had a layer of humanity the Agency wouldn't have tolerated if you let it show."

"You know, Sandra, I do appreciate your helping me walk through this, but I would be grateful if you could be a little more gentle in talking about it. Maybe a little more like my loving wife than my shrink.

"I don't know how much it has to do with the surprise of finding Andy the friend I remember from so long ago. There's probably a part of me that hopes this might help me exorcise the ghost of Rick Ames. Though I can't see any good reason for wanting to feel any different about that asshole.

"I admit I would probably bail on this without you to keep egging me on. The whole thing's got me tied in knots. I'm not at all sure this is a good idea. I feel like if I'd ever let this squishy part of me see daylight when I was working for the Agency, I'd be under dirt or in jail. I keep thinking that wanting to make things different now that I'm a civilian again is wishful, risky, stupid thinking. Is all this being driven by the kind of wish for approval and love we were trained to guard against by the Agency?"

Sandra stifled a laugh. "Sweet Jesus, Max, you never cease to amaze me. Tough, old, grizzled spy who did shit that would make most people's stomach erupt, and here you are opening yourself to something that takes more courage than running one of your agents. And you're worried it makes you a wuss.

"If I seem to be making sport, it's only because it makes me a little jumpy too. But even more it makes me proud of you. I'm so glad you didn't dry up and die inside from having to keep yourself so tightly wrapped all those years."

She pulled him into an embrace and planted a big kiss directly on his lips.

"Should have tried this years ago," Max laughed.

"Weird," Sandra said as they relaxed their embrace, "but I found myself wondering how much all this has to do with Andy being a priest and your looking for absolution for some of the stuff you worry might be unforgivable. Do you think you'd even consider doing this if Andy wasn't a priest?"

"I've wondered about that, too," Max said. "You know I believe my faith is what kept me together so many times when it seemed like the wheels were about to come off. Especially those times my job required something of me I would ordinarily think wrong. Immoral. Sinful. I haven't got a good read yet on what Andy's being a priest has to do with all that. But it's got to be a factor."

From: **andy@gmail.com**
To: **maxman@comcast.net**
Subject: Great!

Thanks for your willingness to give it a whirl, Max, despite what we both understand is a pretty big issue stuck in our common craw. I am no better than you at the friendship thing. My 30 years as a parish priest were effective antidote to close relationships. (Ask Alice!) Yes, I remember our time as boys being as much friendship as I have experienced with anyone. I felt that upbeat energy rise like the Phoenix from the ashes when we met at your place. I don't know whether it made me more excited or anxious. I will make reservations at The Palms At Indian Head in Borrego for Tuesday, January 12, leaving Friday the 15th. It takes a little more than two hours to the airport so you can make a flight back Friday, anytime from about noon on. It's a funky old motel where Hollywood actors used to go for trysts. What I like about it in addition to being simple and quiet, is you can walk from there into the trail to the palm oasis.

Rumor has it that Clark Gable spent time there with Marilyn Monroe. So far as I know JFK never got there.

Max immediately emailed a response in which he said that despite his misgivings the Marilyn Monroe story persuaded him, and the place sounded great.

~

In the six weeks between their email exchanges and Andy picking up Max at Lindbergh field in San Diego, both men mentally ran the tape on their very different histories with Aldrich Ames, with some wise, if uninvited, help from their wives.

~

"Oh shit!" Andy exclaimed before he was even totally awake. Alice sat up, looking down at him still prone beside her.

"What does that mean?" she asked.

"What does what mean?" Andy asked, awake but not fully oriented.

"You just said, 'Oh shit.'"

"I did? I was dreaming. Rick and I were playing hand ball. I hit a high shot against the front wall and he clipped me with his elbow when he tried to pick it off the back wall. Pissed me off."

"You have the best dreams," she said. "What in the world do you make of that one?"

"Oh God," Andy said, rubbing sleep from his eyes, "these days all I think about is that miserable Rick Ames and what I'm going to say about our friendship when I meet Max."

"You're really nervous about going to Borrego with Max, aren't you."

"Boy, you said it. Wish I'd never gotten back together with him." Andy threw his leg over the side of the bed. His thinning hair stood up straight. He caught sight of himself in the mirror. *I look like a deranged old man who's been living on the street.* "I just can't believe I let myself get so involved with Ames. I used to consider myself a decent judge of character."

"And you are," Alice tried to reassure him. "How many times have I heard you encourage someone who has a hate on for someone else, to try to learn what that other person is wrestling with before writing him off? And how it so often turns out that something about him makes you look at something about yourself that makes you uncomfortable?"

Andy stood up, staggered a little as his foot caught the edge of the rug. "That's the trouble with making your living giving out public advice that can be used against you when you don't take the advice yourself."

Alice sat up. "Andy, you know I wasn't criticizing you. That's still great advice even if it's so hard to consider it good now. I bet if you'd known the pressures Rick was under you might still wish you hadn't let yourself become such a good friend, but you might not beat yourself up so much for not seeing through him. What I remember about all that is, even as hurt and angry as you were when Rick was arrested, you still had compassion for him. Despite the public pressure you agreed to be a character witness. That took courage."

"Kind of you, Alice, but I don't think I want to let myself off that hook. The man is an unprincipled wretch who made a fool of me. There's no softening it."

"Just one more reminder, Andy, from one of your most memorable sermons, and I promise I'll leave you alone. 'When you can't forgive someone, it's because you haven't forgiven yourself.' Sound familiar?"

Andy grunted, went into the bathroom, sat on the toilet and released his full bladder in a long pee. *When did I start sitting to pee?*

That morning he emailed Stuart Morris, a former parishioner, the lawyer who represented Aldrich Ames.

From: **andy@gmail.com**
To: **stuartm@laxlaw.org**
Subject: Aldrich Ames

Stuart, after Rick Ames went to prison you told me you might be able to get through by email if I ever wanted to communicate with him. At the time I didn't think I'd ever want that. Lately I've been thinking about it and I just might like to have a brief exchange if you think it's possible. And so long as you don't think it might catch the eye of whatever today's equivalent of the House Un-American Activities Committee is. I know you didn't like representing him any better than I liked testifying as a character witness, but I admired the professional and kind way you handled it.

Thanks for considering this. And for becoming an even better handball opponent than Rick was. This morning I dreamed he hit me in the jaw with his elbow while returning my shot.

Andy

From: **stuartm@laxlaw.org**
To: **andy@gmail.com**
Subject: Aldrich Ames

I am able to email with Aldrich so long as he is legitimately my client. He's forbidden to email with anyone else except his wife, but it's OK for me to forward a question or comment, so long as you don't mind it being read by the feds. Not exactly a pastoral setup, but maybe better than nothing? Let me know.

I would say Rick hit you somewhere lower than your jaw, when he went from best friend, doubles partner and godfather to Amy, to traitor. Hate to admit, but he was a better handball player than I was.

Aside from the terrible thing he did I actually quite liked the guy. I always had, and when he asked me to represent him, I hoped he'd been framed. Afraid not. Getting him life rather than death, which was what the prosecutor wanted, was the best we could do.

Hope you and Alice and Amy have a Merry Christmas, and that we might find a way to get together in the coming year.

Stuart

From: **andy@gmail.com**
To: **stuartm@laxlaw.com**
Subject: Ames

If you think it appropriate, Stuart, I would be grateful if you could forward this to Ames. I have a specific reason which I look forward to sharing with you one day.

Rick: (Kindness of Stuart Morris) If you're willing, I would like to ask you to answer a few questions that have been plaguing me. 1) Was your part in the parish—Senior Warden, Treasurer, Lay Eucharistic Minister, Lay Reader—part of your spy cover, or sincere? 2) When we asked you to be Amy's godfather were you already involved in counter espionage? 3) If you are willing, as your pastor and once close friend, I would be so grateful if you would tell me why you did what you did and if it weighs on your conscience now? Wish I could say I'm looking for a way to grant you absolution. The Episcopal Church gives me that authority, but not Uncle Sam. Thanks in advance if you're willing to respond. If not I guess I can understand. Hope prison isn't as bad as I know it can be. Andy

From: **stuartm@laxlaw.org**
To: **andy@gmail.com**
Subject: Ames

I've sent your email to the agency through which I communicate with Aldrich Ames, Andy. I spoke with the woman who handles these things and she said while there's no prohibition against doing this, the censors at the prison can get pretty arbitrary about what gets through. Even if it does, there's no knowing if he'll respond. So don't get your hopes up too high. I confess I'd love to know your motivation if you ever feel like telling me. Sorry that any response will have to go through me, if there is a response. Wish I could tell you I'm so principled I wouldn't read it before passing it on. I'm not, and it might be helpful the next time I have a national traitor for a client. Oh, the tangled web, Andy, as you know all too well from your long useful career as pastor.

Stuart

Andy tried to put the email issue with Rick Ames out of his mind, but the three weeks between when Stuart Morris told him he'd sent it, and the time he got a response, he found it hard to think about anything else.

From: **aames@jpay.com**
To: **stuartm@laxlaw.org**
Re: Andy Coffer

In the nearly three years since I arrived in this place I have only communicated with family and you. Maybe I'm ready to venture further, though I wonder how lenient the censors will be. Here are partial answers to Andy's questions:

1) My part in church and in your life were in no way cover. I am a lifelong Episcopalian and my sense of why that mattered to me deepened during that time. You and Alice had a lot to do with that.

2) My treachery began sometime after (and unrelated) to your asking me to be Amy's godfather. I felt deeply undeserving, but I love Amy and wanted to do it. I understand that beneath those questions there is your wanting to know why I did what I did. Prison offers more time than one wants to consider those questions, and I have. I'm not ready yet to try that out on anyone. I still haven't exorcised my wish to rationalize it in some way that makes it seem not so awful. I will, I hope, and then maybe we can communicate further. I never had a chance to tell you how sorry I am about betraying you, the one friend whose trust really mattered to me.

Hope you're OK, and if it seems appropriate, give love to Alice. And to Amy.

Rick

Andy's feelings were all over the map as he read Rick's email, forwarded by Stuart without comment. He briefly considered forwarding it on to Max, but after mentioning it to Alice, didn't.

"Andy," she said, "if it were me, I wouldn't even want Max to know I'd communicated with Rick, until you two have had a face-to-face about the weird fact of your friendship you revealed to him after your meeting."

Amy came home to Vermont for Christmas from New York. She had recently been made partner in the downtown law firm in which she had been an associate since graduating from NYU Law School six years earlier.

One late afternoon Andy and Amy cross-country skied across the pond, through the woods on the other side, and up a few hills that now challenged Andy more than they once did. When they got home the sun was already low. Andy mustered just enough energy to build a fire. Alice made some hot mulled cider and the three of them sat in front of the fire as the sun sank behind the hills that sheltered the town burial ground across the road from the house.

"So sweet to be out of the New York rat race for a few days," Amy said as her mother handed her a mug. "I always wanted to be made partner but I never bothered to consider how much crazier it would make my life. You two sure hit the jackpot when you decided to retire to rural Vermont."

Andy smiled. "When I was your age I was filled with energy and ambition. Had you showed me a picture of us sitting here like this I would have thought this life might bore me."

"There are days when I'd kill to be bored," Amy said.

"I've been in touch just a little, indirectly, with your god-father," Andy said, as he poked the logs to make the fire burn hotter.

"Rick Ames?" Amy asked.

"Uh huh." Andy continued poking the fire, his back to her. "I don't know if you remember Stuart Morris, but he was Aldrich's lawyer, and he is allowed to be middleman. It isn't much but Aldrich did ask specifically to send his love to you."

Andy put the poker back in its stand and lowered himself into the cushioned easy chair, grunting as his weary legs relaxed. Amy stared at the fire, silent for several minutes. Alice looked around the corner from the kitchen wondering how she was going to respond.

"You know, Dad, I do think about him more often than you might imagine. He was a sort of uncle to me during those years I was an adolescent. I don't think my confusion is so much about what he did, though, even after all these years I can't imagine what possessed him, but about whether his affection and attention was real, or part of his cover. Was I a jerk to consider him such an important person in my life?"

Andy sighed. Alice stayed in the kitchen, silent, listening.

"I know," Andy said, "that's pretty much what I asked him in the email. Not so much about you, but about our friendship and his very central role in the church and in our lives."

"What'd he say?"

Andy got up from his chair, picked up the poker, pushed the logs around some more. "Not a lot. He said his part in our lives and as your godfather were genuine to him, not fake. And that his treachery—that's the word he used—had begun after all that."

"Do you believe him?" Amy asked, her father's back to her as he continued fiddling with the fire.

"I don't know, Amy. I haven't been able to sort out what this is all about for me. There's a reason this comes up now."

"Oh?"

Andy leaned the poker against the wall and sat, again grunting. "Last month my class at Salisbury had its 50th reunion. I didn't go, but a guy who'd been my closest friend at the American School in Manila, who'd also gone to Salisbury for those two years, was on the list they sent us, and we communicated. Each other's oldest friend in life. I went to see him."

Andy took in a big breath. "His name is Max and he turns out to have been one of the most highly decorated under-cover agents in the history of the CIA."

"Holy shit!" Amy said.

"I know," said Andy.

"Max and I made an amazing reconnection when I went to spend some time with him and his wife at their place hidden away on top of a mountain in the Shenandoah Valley. We hadn't seen each other in 50 years. It was as if we'd just shot hoops together."

"And what about him and Rick?" Amy asked impatiently.

"We didn't talk about it," Andy admitted.

"You got together with your closest childhood friend, discovered you still love each other as you did then. Your once closest adult friend is in prison for betraying the CIA. Your childhood friend spent his life with the CIA? And you didn't mention it?"

Silence.

"No. Honestly, or as honest as I can be with myself about this, I didn't think of it until nearly the end of my visit. And then I just couldn't bear to bring it up."

"But he did finally email Max and tell him," Alice interjected as she came in from the kitchen. "I think it was incredibly hard for your father to do that."

"Man, I guess," Amy said. "Talk about drama. Where do things stand now?"

"Max and I agreed this wasn't something we could deal with long distance. So, soon after we go back to San Diego for winter he is flying out and we'll go to Borrego for a few days."

"Good old Borrego," Amy said. "The sacred ground from whom no secrets are hid."

~ ~ ~

XXI

After a six-inch snowfall, Max shoveled off the deck from which he could see maybe 50 miles to the peaks of several mountains.

"How about we have breakfast out here?" he called to Sandra, who was grinding coffee in the kitchen.

"Suits me," she answered, "so long as it isn't bitter cold."

"Sun's already warming it up, no wind, and if we're still and quiet I bet we have a chance of seeing that bear.

"You know what's bugging me?" Max asked after they'd finished the bacon and eggs and were drinking their coffee while looking out over the valley.

"Yes, I think I might, but why don't you tell me."

"What if Andy tries to persuade me that his old friend Rick Ames is really a sweet fellow who was really a good guy who just made a mistake and I'd really like him if I understood him?"

"Max," she said, shaking her head, "do you think Andy is dumb, or clueless? Why would be do something like that?"

"For the same reason I've agreed to go to the desert with him. He's a priest. It's his job to forgive people. I'd like to believe he actually has the power to forgive me for shit I did that haunts me. Why wouldn't he do the same for Ames. And probably think I should too?"

"And what if he does do that?"

"I think I'd choke the bastard."

Sandra laughed. "Right, and that, among other reasons is why Andy would never do such a thing.

"Besides looking for a clean slate with God, what is the reason you agreed to go with him to the desert?"

"You're the only person who knows how truly scared I am of having to spend eternity in hell," Max admitted. "I think that would be reason enough. I'm not sure I think Andy, or the Pope, or God can ever really forgive me.

"I'm going because I just loved talking with Andy in ways I hadn't with anyone for as far back as I can remember. It started to come pretty easily.

"And maybe he can absolve me."

"What about with me? Even if I can't absolve you, I love you even knowing the things you're scared about," Sandra said. "And you talk pretty easily to me."

"You don't count. I don't even have to use words for you to know what's going on with me. Sometimes that's as big a burden as it is a blessing."

"Fuck you, and thank you," Sandra said, smiling, but not laughing.

"Oh get real," Max said. "You understand what I mean."

"I do. Still, it's a little jarring."

"Sorry, I didn't mean it to be."

"I think you're getting warmed up for a new kind of conversation in that desert with Andy."

"I don't know. Talk about teaching an old dog new tricks. You were the one who warned me against easing up on those hard-earned disciplines we learned, just because we're old and lonely." Long pause. "And afraid to die."

"There's no doubt that'll be a challenge, Max, remembering how to hold that line between an exciting new, old friendship and all that stuff that must never escape your lips in your lifetime. I would think Andy's being a priest could blur that fine line."

Max looked out to the horizon. He stood up, picked up his plate, then put Sandra's on top of his.

"I'll do the dishes," he said.

"Sweet, thanks," she said. She watched him carry them inside to the kitchen, noticing how he favored his left leg, that old injury from the attack that nearly cost him his life.

I hope Andy's as sensitive and smart as I think, she thought.

~~~

XXII

For 15 years Andy and Alice had migrated semi-annually between their Vermont farmhouse and the small apartment in San Diego. Hartford, an hour and a half drive from home, a plane change in Dallas, another three hours to Lindbergh Field, San Diego was always a time for Andy to run through things that were hanging fire, things that remained unfocused.

How long would their money and their patience with increasingly burdensome air travel, heavy San Diego traffic, and offensive over-the-top southern California money worship, hold out?

There's tennis, Andy thought, *though a pretty poor cousin to the tennis I remember as a younger man. There's the ocean, the womb my unconscious remembers as my original home. And endless sunny days, though the decades-long drought may make life untenable. I do love going to the desert, it gives me a visceral sense of some of the stories about the prophets and Jesus.*

The culture is tough for me, pretty detached from reality. Not like poor, rural Vermont, where you feel so much a part of nature it sometimes seems you're planted alongside the vegetables that feed us all summer. Living out of our garden, being across the road from the burial ground where those who have lived in our house before us are buried, just feels somehow in proportion. Southern California, if I'm anywhere except immersed in the great Pacific womb, feels all out of human dimension.

On the second leg of the trip, over the snow covered Rockies, Andy's mood shifted from his chronic confusion about where he belonged, to what to expect when he and Max went to the desert after the first of the year.

Why am I doing this? What's in it for me? What ever made me think Rick Ames was someone I wanted as a close friend? How fucked up is it to think reconnecting with Max is going to get me anywhere but right back into those nasty days after Ames was arrested?

His mind went back to that night. The phone rang at 3 A.M. He dreaded those middle of the night calls. He immediately recognized Rick's voice. His mind raced, wondering what disaster prompted him to call at 3 A.M.

"Andy, it's Rick."

Andy grunted acknowledgment, waiting for the other shoe to drop.

"I'm in trouble."

What kind of trouble can't wait 'till morning?

"The FBI came to my house and arrested me. Nancy and Maria watched as they took me away in handcuffs. I'm being held in the county jail."

The county jail was just down the street from the rectory where Andy and Alice lived.

"You want me to come bail you out?" *Jesus, Andy,* he thought, *the FBI arrested him; this isn't a DUI.*

"No, you can't. I called Stuart Morris before I called you. He told me not to say anything to anyone until he got here in the morning. But I had to call you."

"What can I do to help?" Andy asked. *Without getting arrested myself.*

"Pray," Aldrich said. "And give support to Nancy and Maria. This is going to be nasty for them."

"Of course," Andy said.

"I've used up my time," Aldrich said. "No idea when we'll talk again. No matter what you hear, whatever happens, you and all you've done for me means more to me than anything. It's going to be hard for you to consider me your friend, or forgive me, but I hope to God you can." Aldrich hung up without waiting for Andy to reply.

At Stuart Morris' pleading Andy did testify, reluctantly, as a character witness when Stuart told him it might be the one thing that would keep him from getting the death penalty. Andy hadn't spoken with Rick again before he pled guilty and was sent to the super max prison in Colorado.

I could have imagined that he'd somehow gotten into the till at the Agency, but never espionage. He was always worried about money but I had him figured for a super-patriot.

He used to rag on me about my anti-war views. Said I lacked patriotism.

I'm embarrassed to admit to myself how much I liked him, even after his second divorce when most of his friends wrote him off. Yeah, I knew he was a womanizer. I probably would have been too if I was braver. And if I weren't a priest.

If I wrote off every otherwise good guy who was an actual or wannabe womanizer in those days my only friends would have been closet gays. Or geeks. He never fit my picture of a CIA guy. I attributed his working there to his father having been with the Agency. Turns out he sure as hell knew how to keep a secret, just from the wrong side.

Wonder what Max thought of Rick before he knew he was a mole? Must be really unnerving, one of your own being a mole, after you've spent your best energy and risked your own life turning the enemy's agents into your moles. This visit with Max could be mega uncomfortable.

~~~

XXIII

"Are you stuck, thinking Andy's going to explain away what Rick did by telling you the stress he was under? And want you to do the same thing?" Sandra asked Max.

Max's head shot up, eyes wide, as if she'd said something unimaginable. "What're you talking about? You think I give a shit what that asshole was thinking when he turned?"

Sandra took her time answering. She, too, had been with the Agency, though not undercover. Managing agents from the enemy side didn't lend itself to being a purist about motivation. Knowing the weird things that succeed in persuading a KGB agent to turn could make even the most obtuse CIA agent uneasy about his own frailties that might make him vulnerable. It would be considered way out of bounds for an Agency officer to try to justify one of your own becoming a double agent.

"Well Max, of course it's not the same," Sandra reassured him. "But no one was more skilled than you at persuading agents, especially KGB agents, to turn and work for us. So maybe you'd get the motivation for turning, even one of ours, better than most would."

Max paced back and forth tilting to one side as he favored his gimp leg, lighting a cigarette while one was still burning in the ash tray.

"The two are in no way comparable, and you know it as well as I do," he said angrily. "Don't try fucking with my mind just because you want me to make better friends with Andy."

"Max, I didn't mean…"

"I know what you meant," he interrupted. "It's more of that weak-minded, liberal bullshit about how once you understand motivations, we and they are all the same. Aldrich Ames is the worst sort of black heart. He took a solemn oath and he violated it. Cost a lot of people a lot of trouble. And more than one, his life. So don't give me that bullshit about how I ought to understand him. If Andy tries any of that understanding and forgiveness shit with me, that'll end it."

Sandra sighed. She'd learned the cost of trying to sort all that out with Max. *This doesn't bode well for the visit,* she thought.

~

Andy's final parish had been in San Diego, and Alice had established a busy interior design practice there. Though both felt more rooted in Vermont, they appreciated the weather and the ocean during San Diego winter.

"I'm not sure how much longer I want to do this," Andy said to her before they flew west this year. "San Diego is great, but the trip is getting harder, and I miss the peace and quiet of Vermont."

"Won't take much to persuade me," Alice responded. She'd loved being stretched by the eclectic design world of the southwest, but her passion for early American furniture and houses meant she never felt quite at home in California.

"Still, I'm glad we're here this year," she said. "I think the Borrego desert is a perfect place for you and Max to sort out whatever it is between you."

~~~

XXIV

Borrego

Andy picked up Max at Lindbergh Field Tuesday afternoon. Pulling up to the curb, Andy noticed Max limped as he rolled his bag toward the car. Andy jumped out to help. Max didn't object when Andy lifted the bag into the trunk. They greeted each other with a handshake. Andy pulled Max into an embrace which Max responded to stiffly at first, then relaxed. They held the embrace which Andy hoped was a positive signal for what lay ahead.

As Max dropped heavily into the passenger seat, he let out a long sigh.

"How was your flight?"

"Long. Exhausting. I wouldn't care if I never flew again."

Andy gave his friend a long look before pulling away from the curb. Lack of color in Max's face, his drawn look, concerned Andy.

"You OK?"

"Yeah, yeah, I'm fine. Just tire easily these days."

Andy wasn't convinced. Another sigh from Max didn't reassure him. "We've got a little more than two hours' drive to Borrego; you OK with that or would you like to bed down with us tonight and drive out tomorrow?"

"The drive's just what the doctor ordered," Max said, with what Andy hoped was a little more energy in his voice. "I hope you won't be offended if I nod off. I don't sleep on planes and I missed my usual morning nap."

"Not at all, man, go for it."

Before they had reached the I-5, five minutes from the airport Max had fallen into deep sleep. His head flopped forward and back, mouth open. He snored loudly. He didn't open his eyes for the next hour and a half until the car's weight began shifting as Andy guided it through the hairpin turns on the descent into the Borrego desert.

Max woke with a start. "What the fuck?!" he said, his voice hoarse. "What... Damn. Oh, sorry," his face a cha-grined smile. "I had no clue where we were. Must have been dreaming. You were some fucking Arab who'd captured me and was taking me somewhere to torture me. Or some-thing." Max snorted a laugh.

Despite Max's laughter, Andy was concerned. "We're headed down the grade into Borrego," he said. "Naïve me. When I suggested coming here I never thought about your

years in the Middle East in places just like this. So dangerous, so scary."

"No worries," Max reassured him. "Those Arabs do a
lot of horrible things to each other in the desert, but since
I'm not a member of any of the rival tribes I never had the
pleasure. In fact I love the desert. The purity, quiet. The ran-
dom violence of snakes and coyotes and scorpions. Unlike
our species it's not personal with them, just what they do to
survive.

"That was something I tried hard to learn," Max went on,
"to do my job without letting it get personal, no matter how
much deceit and violence it required. Best spies never let
themselves be led by their anger."

Andy was silent, concentrating on navigating the twist-
ing turns, considering what Max said. He wondered at the
irony, spies who cheated and lied and slit throats, exercising
emotional discipline.

"I was just thinking about all the gossip sessions I've been
part of," Andy said. They were often dedicated to plots of
revenge against slights, real and imagined. Guess I shouldn't
be surprised that spies are more disciplined, less vengeful
than clergy."

Max seemed to have regained his energy. He let out a
belly laugh. "I didn't say spies don't get mad and don't care
about revenge. I meant when spying requires lying, or
doing great harm to someone you may not have a personal
beef with, you have to set aside whatever emotional issues
you may have, or you're going to make bad, maybe deadly,
mistakes."

Dusk was settling over the desert. Each time they came around one of the sharp curves they could see Borrego's lights begin to twinkle.

"Beautiful," Max said. "Imagine the rabbits that are going to provide feasts for coyotes before the sun bakes the desert again."

Andy laughed. "You appreciate beauty in ways I might never have thought of."

"The fun's just beginning," Max said.

Neither spoke again until they pulled out of the final turn onto the desert floor. At the intersection of the main road to the town Andy pulled up to the stop sign, then went straight ahead onto a remote road barely two lanes wide. The road, sand blown, curved this way and that, deserted except for an occasional small adobe dwelling. The darkness had deepened. There were no street lights. All that was visible was what the headlights briefly illuminated.

"Jesus Andy, I'm thinking my dream might have been more than a dream. Where are you taking me?"

"You know, Max, I'm seeing all this as if for the first time, through your eyes," Andy laughed. The Borrego desert's an oasis for me, respite from the frustrations that some days seemed all there was to parish life. I'm seeing how menacing it might be to someone who had a pretty different kind of job."

Maybe this was a bad idea. The desert is like a perfect reminder of everything he had to guard against. Could be just about the last place we should talk about anything that's scary. Like Rick Ames.

~~~

XXV

"You feeling refreshed?" Andy asked Max after they'd had some time in their rooms. They were seated in the small restaurant at the motel, looking at a large, lighted pool. "Just beyond that pool," Andy said, "is the remnant of an air strip from the days when Hollywood stars used this place as a getaway. Usually for a tryst. Maybe that's where Clark Gable landed when he brought Marilyn Monroe here."

Max laughed. "I can sure see how they could stay out of sight here. If it weren't for the pool lights and a few twinkling lights on the slopes of those mountains way off there you might think you were on the moon. Reminds me of 29 Palms in the Mojave, where we sometimes went to join the Marines for survival training."

Andy took a sip of his Tequila. "You did survival training?"

"Well, yeah, despite our foolhardy reputation, spies are just as interested in surviving as everyone.

"Am I feeling refreshed? The long nap on the drive here—apologies for being lousy company—was just what I needed. Feeling pretty good and this martini is going to make me feel even better."

Andy looked around at people at surrounding tables. None were within hearing range. "I was wondering if we want to jump right in, or wait until we've had a night's sleep. I can go either way."

Max looked off into the dark desert before responding. "I'm not sure what you have in mind when you talk about jumping in, but I'd welcome a chance to catch up a little before we get into the heavy stuff, assuming you're talking about Aldrich Ames."

"I'm in for that," Andy answered. "A lot of water's gone over the dam since we were kids in Manila. What really struck me when we got together at your house was how much being with you felt the way I remember feeling back then. Maybe we could take some time now to tell about stuff that has marked us along the way.

"I mean, being a spy can't just be business as usual. And I daresay being a priest has its weird moments.

"I don't kid myself that we're the same people we were then. You mentioned that you've undergone multiple surgeries. Is that because of something that happened to you, or chronic illness?"

"They have to keep operating on me is because of that stuff I told you about that happened in Tehran right after the Shah was overthrown. My job was to get the Savak guys—in reality our guys we trained and paid to protect the Shah—out of the country before they were executed by the Revolutionary Guard.

"They weren't the first dead guys I'd ever seen, but I can't say I'd ever been happier to see guys dead.

"I staggered back to my quarters. Pissed, shit and vomited blood for three days. Couldn't eat. Forced myself to get out of bed a couple of times each day, knowing I was a candidate for pneumonia or worse."

"Good Lord, Max, what did the CIA do about that?"

"Nothing. I didn't tell them. If I had, they would have removed me from country immediately and I had several more Savak guys I was responsible for getting out of country.

"You know most things, even horrendous things, get better if they don't kill you. I recovered enough to carry on with getting more Savak guys out, and hung on with the Agency for a couple more decades. I always knew some things inside me weren't right.

"Ten years ago the chronic pain became acute and I went to see a doc. When he examined me he said he'd never seen a live person with so many organs and body parts in the wrong places.

"What's a real pisser is that I can't get a penny of compensation for the medical care. Thank God for Medicare, because the Agency denied my requests for them to pick

up a share for disability. Despite using every connection—
Congress members, Senators, a former Secretary of State—
who interceded for me."

"What the fuck, Max?"

"My sentiments exactly. The Agency has its rules, might
bend them for extracting information now and then, but
not for paying me. I knew it was required to report injuries
within two weeks of their occurrence, or they would not be
considered injuries incurred in the line of duty."

"OK," Andy said, "rules I understand, but you were nearly
killed in the line of duty. Rules are meant to work for us, not
against us. When events make the rules nonsense, change
the rules. My boss, Jesus, said something like, 'Rules were
made for the benefit of humans, not humans for the benefit
of rules.'"

Andy heard the scorn in Max's laugh.

"You Jesus types think the rules can just be changed
when they don't suit you. What is it you call that: situational
ethics? The Agency doesn't do situational ethics. Live by the
sword, die by the sword."

Now it was Andy's turn to laugh. "I can't believe you
know about situation ethics. The guy who first came up
with that was my Ethics professor in seminary, Joe Fletcher.
Joseph McCarthy hauled him before his committee and
accused him of being a communist because he used to go
to international ethics meetings in eastern Europe, attended
by communists. When Senator McCarthy asked him if he
had ever been a member of the Communist Party, instead
of answering, Joe looked across at the senator and said,
'Senator, the question isn't why some people were members

of the Communist Party during those dark days, but why *everyone* wasn't.'"

"Good for him," Max said. "McCarthy was a prick. But I still believe a code of behavior has to be sustained, even when it seems cruel, arbitrary. Start fudging the rules, even when it seems more fair, and you're quickly into the nasty chaos of expediency. Squishy feelings. Fact is, if you really want to know, it's probably the reason, as much as anything, why I believe in God. Somebody has to make rules that apply to everyone, everywhere. God makes the rules. When we follow them things go well. When we don't, you can bet the shit's going to hit the fan."

That set off an alarm in Andy. All that stood between him and hanging up his clerical collar all those years was Jesus' counterintuitive teaching, the opposite of a code of ethics. Andy thought Jesus (if there really was such a person), mainly meant to counter rigid Pharisaical Judaism. To stand against rules when they did damage to people rather than serve them.

I'm going to think about that a little more before trying to explain it to Max. Too soon. How often I've drilled a hole in a promising friendship by trying to make sense of this! Freaks people out.

Max's experience as a spy made him alert to what's not getting said in a conversation. He twisted in his seat, reached for a Marlboro from the pack on the table beside him. Andy already had come to understand this as a signal that Max was feeling antsy.

"If it weren't for the Ten Commandments this nasty world would be a lot nastier," Max insisted. If I didn't believe the Ten Commandments mattered enough to protect with my life, I doubt I would have spent all those years in the Agency."

Andy let out a deep sigh. How many times he'd had a replica of this conversation with skeptical parishioners. He'd become skilled at finessing it. It frustrated him that he was so seldom able to get through to people with whom he otherwise felt in tune, how much this picture of Jesus as subversive of conventional morality was key to his picture of what Jesus was up to.

Andy began slowly, tentatively. "The Ten Commandments is an ancient tribal code that has maintained its authority because it is general enough to apply to most things we humans face. And because it is consistent with most other western codes of ethics.

"The striking thing about the Jesus movement,"—Andy really hated trying to explain this part, so easily misconstrued—"and the reason the Roman Empire considered the Jesus movement subversive until Constantine co-opted it for his own use, was because it dares to claim that God's love trumps all the rules. The charge against Jesus was treason. Violating the code."

Max shifted in his chair. With the Zippo Andy had returned to him he lit the cigarette that had been hanging from his lip.

"You mean like Aldrich Aims?" Max asked.

Andy's eyebrows shot up. This was exactly how he did not want to broach this subject. He shrugged his shoulders, intending to signal that he chose to remain silent. He waited for more.

Max said, "My biggest responsibility, my greatest success with the agency was turning KGB agents, guys with access to the specs for the anti-aircraft guns around the lake in downtown Hanoi that were bringing down so many of our planes. Those guns were supplied by the Soviets and they were damned good. They delivered John McCain to the Hanoi Hilton.

"I had made friends with a guy in their embassy in D.C. We used to have lunch together and talk about football."

"Football with a KGB agent?"

"Turns out he knew a lot more about the Redskins and the Dallas Cowboys than I did. He called them America's Team. Dawned on me that anyone with those passions likely had developed a taste for things American.

"To cut to the chase, he ended up providing me with the specs for those guns. He got them from fellow dissidents in Moscow. Surprised me how many there were who hated their system so much they were willing to take this giant risk.

"And for nearly a year and a half, they didn't bring down a single one of our planes. I felt like the best spy the CIA ever had and my superiors did nothing to discourage my feeling.

"One day one of our planes was shot down by a missile that seemed to have a different trajectory from any our flyboys had ever seen. When I next saw my KGB agent I asked him about it.

"'Just bad luck,' he insisted, and on my way home I dropped his money in the trash basket where he'd find it, our long-standing arrangement. Two weeks went by without another plane being brought down, and I believed he'd told me the truth. Though the part about the different trajectory still gave me pause.

"Then another was shot down and when I confronted him he looked distressed. I pushed and he finally confided to me that one of those back in Moscow who had been feeding him information had disappeared. Neither of us said what we both knew it had to mean.

"Two more agents in Moscow disappeared before my guy also was suddenly no longer in the embassy. Turns out the last specs he gave me were dummies, meant to throw us off. From then until the end of the war, our guys were on their own for those runs over Hanoi. And we lost a lot of them.

"I never knew what had happened until 20 years later Aldrich Aims was arrested and charged with espionage. He had tipped them off to my guy, and the guys he was working with were executed. So, I'm sure, was my guy. They let him keep on with me just long enough to expose the moles who were giving him the information."

As Max told the story, Andy wished he could crawl into a hole. He knew what was coming.

Max's eyes narrowed and his face turned crimson. "So, you're telling me that Aldrich Aims and Jesus were the same kind of holy men. Traitors to their own kind. That could sure shoot a big hole in my religious convictions."

As Max told his story, something from Andy's life came vividly to his mind, so distracting that Max's angry, sarcastic comparison of Jesus and Aldrich Ames went right by him. It didn't register.

"Max, I've got a big admission to make. May be a deal breaker." Andy paused, looked down at his feet, took a swallow of water. "While you were turning KGB agents to keep those guns from bringing down our planes, I was junior curate in my first job. And I became Chairman of the Summit County, Ohio Committee for Peace in Vietnam. I led the anti-war movement in southern Ohio for three years, the very same years you were just talking about.

Max stamped out his mostly un-smoked cigarette in the metal ashtray next to his recliner. He stared at Andy in disbelief.

"Now you're fucking with me, Andy."

"No, Max, I'm afraid I'm telling you the truth."

"Well, I'll be," Max said. "My best friend." He laughed a deep, husky, smoker's laugh. "Jesus Christ, Andy, our lives didn't disconnect 50 years ago the way we thought, did they? We've been tightly connected, but in convoluted ways no novelist would dare invent."

Andy wasn't sure whether he was reading Max right. He didn't seem enraged. *Maybe even in some weird way he's enjoying the irony.* They both laughed, nervously at first. Their chuckling grew, until they were roaring laughter. They rose from their chairs and fell into each other's arms, laughing, choking tears.

They stepped back, arms on each other's shoulders looking at each other as if they were seeing themselves in a carnival fun mirror. They struggled to take in what they had just uncovered.

"I'll tell you something, Andy. You were politically, maybe even morally, right in wanting us to end that debacle. But I still think you're a fucking Commie traitor." Max laughed harder, began to choke.

Andy and Max again fell on each other's neck, embracing, choking, laughing, tears running down their cheeks.

"I'd say we've covered about as much ground as I can manage for one session," Andy said, after they both regained some of their composure. "What say we turn in and start again in the morning when we're both fresh. I don't know about you but the crackers and cheese we've been snacking on are as much dinner as I need."

"Same for me," Max said. "I've had way more than I can process in one sitting. "Whether I'll sleep much and be fresh in the morning is problematic. But yes, let's adjourn for the night."

Weary from the long drive and the emotional discovery of their weirdly connected roles during the Vietnam War, Andy and Max each left the sliding glass doors to their rooms open so the desert air could work its magic. Like most their age they normally slept fitfully. That night neither even got up to pee.

~ ~ ~

XXVI

They ate breakfast on the patio overlooking the pool. The morning was clear, cool enough that each wore a sweater. After the waiter cleared their plates and poured a second cup of coffee, Max turned toward Andy.

"Before I fell asleep last night, I found myself wondering how a priest decides his vocation is about more than selling Jesus. How come you got tied up in politics? I think I get the God and Jesus part, but I'm not having a lot of luck with the anti-war and Ames part. I could use some help with that."

Andy hesitated. "You in for a kind of long story?"

"I am if it helps me understand the religion and politics thing. That's a big problem for me. Seems like somewhere along the way anti-war and civil rights politics replaced belief in Jesus."

"Ok, pal, settle in," Andy said.

"The Sunday before I began seminary, in Cambridge, Massachusetts, Dad and I—he lived nearby then—went to Christ Church, the colonial Episcopal Church that looks onto the Cambridge Common.

"I think the congregation, coats and ties, hats and dresses, buoyed Dad's confidence that I was making a sensible career choice. The congregation was all closer to Dad's age. It made me wonder what it would be like to spend my life blessing the status quo. But I'd had a couple of pretty intense experiences of what I understood as God, so I was pretty determined to go through with it.

"The board outside the church listed The Rev. John Snow, the assistant minister, as the preacher that day, rather than Dr. Day, the rector. 'Too bad,' Dad said.

"John Snow slouched into the pulpit. His posture seemed an apology for not being Gardiner Day. As he began in his high-pitched, nasal monotone, oh yeah, sermon time, my mind slipped into neutral.

"'I got back last night from Washington, D.C.,' Snow began, 'where I went with a group from this parish to take part in the march on Washington, called and led by The Rev. Martin Luther King, Jr.'

"My mind popped out of neutral. I sensed Dad's, and the others' around us did also.

"For the next half hour in that nasal monotone Snow described in clinical detail what he had seen and heard. And most compelling of all, how it had affected his feelings. (Yes, an Episcopal priest speaking in a sermon about his feelings.) He spoke of feelings about the broken promises of America to her black citizens and feelings of personal shame for having been willing, however unwittingly, to reap the benefits of being born white and socially privileged.

"And how he realized what he was experiencing was like what the disciples experienced when they heard Jesus talk about justice for those who were oppressed.

"When the service was over, the congregation filed out of the church in near total silence. None of the cocktail chatter you're used to hearing at your family church.

"Dad and I shook hands with John Snow at the door. I wanted to thank him, not only for being brave, but also for actually preaching a sermon that mattered. Just as I began to speak I unexpectedly had to choke back a sob. John Snow looked embarrassed. Dad, probably more embarrassed than Snow, quickly filled in, grasping the minister's hand. 'Thank you,' he said, 'your sermon was very—awkward pause, searching for the word—'meaningful.'

"'Kind of you,' Snow responded. It seemed to me he looked even more embarrassed by Dad's banal attempt to say something real, but polite.

"Dad and I walked back toward the seminary. 'What'd you think?' Dad asked me.

"I said I didn't think I was up to the standard that man just set in that sermon. I said I felt like maybe I should try to get a job with Procter & Gamble. I realized as soon as that was out of my mouth that I had thoughtlessly disrespected my father's career.

"'Oops, sorry, Dad,' I said, wanting to repair the slight, 'I didn't mean that quite how it came out. Not that P&G doesn't count. Just it's probably a better fit with how I've been raised than being a prophet. I don't think I have big enough balls.'

"Dad laughed. 'Takes some pretty good-size balls to sell soap in this commercial, dog-eat-dog world, but I understand. That was a pretty stunning 30 minutes.'"

As Andy described that day, Max had a quizzical expression.

"You *do* know, don't you, Andy, that besides a couple of people who kept me alive for those four years in that Jap concentration camp, and of course the Lieutenant who carried me out of Los Baños, your dad was maybe the biggest influence in shaping my life?"

Andy's surprised expression said that no, he hadn't known.

"Of anyone I ever knew he was the clearest example of a man being comfortable with authority, using it not only to succeed in his work, but to care for his family and community. Still is.

"Every big move I ever made—college, marriage, kids, the Agency—I tried to imagine what your dad would think."

Andy was stunned. "No, I had no idea."

"Not that I ever considered business—I knew I'd be terrible—but more how to conduct myself as a man. Nobody, none of the big wigs I've encountered—and that would include Secretaries of State, members of Congress, and a few Presidents—has struck me as a better role model for how to live a life of integrity, a life that counts, than your dad."

Max and Andy sat in silence. Andy felt disoriented.

I've just confessed to Max that I was working against the war he was risking his life for and he laughed and hugged me.

Now he tells me Dad was his role model. Even for joining the CIA. Dad sold soap, for Christ's sake.

"Guess that's one of those deals, a prophet is not without honor save in his own country," Andy said. "I loved him, respected him, feared him, never felt like I lived up to whatever he might have wished for me. I would never in a million years have guessed he played any part in the way you lived your life."

"Well he did," Max said. "And when I found out you had become a minister I figured he must have had the same kind of influence on you."

Andy shifted uncomfortably in his seat. This was shaky ground for him.

"When I first thought about it," Andy said, "probably knowing Dad would approve was a piece of it. But something in me really didn't want to be part of the corporate world like he was. Not even the church corporate world but I guess I pretty much was. I knew plenty of ministers—the ones you'd probably consider successful—spent their ministries blessing and toadying up to the successful corporate world. But it was a couple of rogues who influenced me to see church as a questioner of all that. A couple of them were rectors of our family's church. Dad considered them eccentric, but they knew which fork to use so he put up with them.

"Yet, until that morning at Christ Church, I didn't think I had the smarts or balls to do what those guys did. Still don't but I've never given up trying.

"I knew Dad thought they were flaky. It was Mom who grooved on them. But something I hadn't known how to really consider for my own life got stirred up in me by

John Snow's preaching about Dr. King and the march on Washington.

"Although you and a lot of others might think I was one of those ministers to the manor born, John Snow and several others like him I met along the way became my model. They were, in fact, well born, but determined to set right injustice, even though it had been in their favor."

Max shook his head. "You've got some explaining to do for me, Andy. When we were kids I knew you marched to a different drummer. Me too. That's probably one of the reasons we liked each other. But I'm not at all sure you and I heard the same drumbeats. What's wrong with the corporate thing? I think I always believed it was at the heart of what's great about this country. Maybe even what I was risking my life to protect."

Andy suddenly felt exhausted, as if someone had let out the plug, draining his energy. He had a headache. His bum knee had stiffened from sitting so long. When he turned his head his neck sounded like breaking glass.

"Max, you and I just wandered into the minefield I felt like I was navigating all those 30 years. I was probably like those KGB guys you turned. I looked like one of the church's corporate in-group, but I was actually trying to chip away at their power. My parishioners believed what you just said you believe: following Jesus means protecting the life we know, against those who want to change it."

"Yeah," Max laughed again, "couldn't put it any better. And you're telling me you were actually working against that. In my world that would make you a counter spy."

Andy sighed. "I need a break. There's still the Aldrich Ames thing. Whether this weird friendship can prosper or should be put back on the shelf until you and I are finally put on the shelf ourselves, probably will depend on how that plays out. And whether you'll be OK with my being a subversive priest."

~~~

XXVIII

Andy had hoped for a hike into Palm Canyon, figuring walking together might grease the wheels for a candid exchange without rancor. But when he saw Max limp toward the car at the airport he quickly realized they wouldn't be hiking. And though dry and tolerable when sitting in the shade, the desert temperature in the sun had already climbed past comfortable.

At their ages, bathroom breaks and a chance to be quiet, reflective, even check email, could easily take most of a morning. They came back together at 11:30 and drove into the small town of Borrego where they settled at a shaded table outside a simple restaurant.

Over a BLT and a bowl of chowder they compared their experiences of stepping down from demanding jobs that had consumed not only energy, but most of their psychic space.

Max started. "Not to jump into the Ames thing with all fours but my recurring nightmare—and it didn't stop when I resigned—was of one of my agents being discovered. It was always horrible when it happened even if it was because the guy was careless or exposed by one of his colleagues. It haunted me to wonder if I might have been careless or done something to cause it.

"If he'd been exposed by something over which I had no control, well, painful as that is that's part of the business. We all understood and accepted that.

"What about you? What kept you from sleeping soundly?" Max asked. "I think if I had been in your line of work, I might have worried about whether my big boss actually existed."

That provoked a belly laugh from them both.

"There were parishioners who I think really believed I had out-loud conversations with God," Andy said. "In English even though God only speaks Hebrew."

"Didn't you?" Max asked between guffaws.

"Well, yes, but I flunked Hebrew in seminary so I never could make out what God was saying."

"Well then, I'd say you were a fucking fraud." A trickle of soup slipped down Max's chin as he laughed.

Andy never knew. When someone had food on his face should he mention it or let it be? He lifted his napkin to his own chin hoping the gesture would alert Max.

"Thanks," Max said as he brushed his chin with his napkin. "But seriously, how did you presume to speak for God? I mean, isn't that what you signed on for?"

"I sure hope not. And I hope to God I never did anything to encourage someone else to think I did. I understood my role to be urging people to pay attention to their insides. Dreams, imaginings, intuition, anything that took a different route from rational thinking."

"Funny, our spy training was unremittingly rational, but everyone understood the best spies have some sixth sense you can't train," Max said.

Andy was aware that Max hadn't lit a cigarette since they left the motel. *Has to be the longest I've ever seen him go without.*

"Well, if I had a nickel for every time someone told me they liked the sermon but didn't understand it, I'd be a rich man."

"Must have frustrated you."

"Actually," Andy responded, "I came to think that meant the sermon worked, although people often told me they liked the sermon when they didn't. But the not understanding part made me at least hope it may have by-passed the left lobe and made its way beneath their consciousness.

"That's the way I composed the sermons I thought worked best. They came from some place in me I hadn't been aware of."

"You must have had clergy nightmares," Max said.

"Oh sure," Andy responded. "The usual: when I looked down at the pulpit lectern the notes were in meaningless gibberish."

"I think I've heard that sermon," Max interjected.

"I've preached it more than once. The other-well known priest nightmare is suddenly realizing you're standing in front of the congregation naked."

"Depending on how well hung you are that might get you elected bishop," Max said.

"I suppose," Andy began, his voice lower, serious. "My closest equivalent to your agent nightmare was the confusion of parishioners mistaking pastoral concern for deeply bonded friendship. The kind we're exploring. The classic case is a couple getting divorced. Like every divorcing couple, they each believe they're on the righteous side. Since you speak for God, you'll certainly be on their side.

"Maybe even worse is when someone comes to you and asks to speak under the seal of the confessional. It was my habit when someone did that to tell them I wouldn't consider myself under the seal if they told me something that I thought keeping confidential would do harm to someone else. They always assumed that was a meaningless caveat, like the agreement you sign when you go to a new web site.

"The handful of times that happened, it turned into a big mess."

"Maybe I should be more cautious about how much I tell you," Max said, lighting a cigarette for the first time in more than an hour.

"I can't speak for spies," Andy answered, "but priests are human beings, making human judgments. And if there's something you wouldn't be comfortable with my knowing, I think you shouldn't."

"Spies can get shot for betraying secrets," Max said. "I always assumed the same was true for priests."

"That we'd get shot?"

"Worse; burn forever in hell."

"Did you ever actually know an Agency spy who was shot for that?" Andy asked, wanting to steer the conversation in a different direction.

"Sure, the Soviets did it routinely. We tend to put our guys in prison for life, if they don't defect. I'm sorry we ever stopped shooting them.

"I sure as hell would have liked to shoot your friend Ames."

"Makes me pretty uncomfortable, Max, for you to call him my friend."

"Well, wasn't he? Senior Warden, your daughter's godfather, squash buddy. Sure sounds like a pretty good friend to me."

"I'm searching for a way to distinguish Rick, the guy who was my friend," said Andy, "from the guy who turned your agents. Because, while I can't deny that he and I were friends—*and maybe Alice a better friend than I would have wished*— I haven't the slightest interest in explaining or defending to you what he did. If my having been his friend is a deal breaker between us, frankly it will break my heart because meeting up with you again has turned out to be a highlight of my old age.

"But I will understand."

Max lit up a second time, took a drag on his Marlboro, focused on somewhere above Andy's head, before responding. "You know what I've been dreading, Andy? I was sure you were going to tell me that, as a good Christian, which I certainly am not, I have to understand and forgive Ames.

"I told Sandra that if you said that, I might kill you." The last of his inhaled smoke exhaled with the word 'you'. "Although I admit I'm terrified that maybe I can't ever be forgiven for some of the shit I've done, I just don't get that we have to forgive everyone, no matter what they did."

Andrew understood from the way Max slumped in his chair that it had taken the last ounce of his energy to own up to that.

"I really appreciate your courage in telling me that, Max. The forgiveness thing vexes me too. The way I have rationalized it is to understand that it's God who can forgive, even what we can't."

"Ok," Max said. "But everyone? God forgives everyone, no matter what?"

Andy smiled, not because he found Max's question simplistic, but because he knew it was always the biggest stumbling block for everyone.

"Look," Andy said, "maybe a bit egotistical, but I figure if God can forgive me for things I did that may not seem very important to anyone else but haunt me every day, then God can forgive anyone."

"Even fucking Aldrich Ames?"

"Don't make me speak for God, Max. I don't think Aldrich Ames deserves to be forgiven for what he did. But

I don't think I deserve to be forgiven for some of what I've done either.

"Unless the Jesus thing is a hoax, a pile of shit the church has foisted off on the world to gain power—which describes way too much of church history..." Andy's voice trailed off at the end of that sentence, as if it raised a new thought.

"If anything about Jesus changes how to measure what matters, then, yes, I guess it's that God can figure out how to set things right even with Aldrich Ames."

Max dropped his cigarette on the ground, crushing it beneath his foot. "Well, old buddy, you just hit this old spy right in the nuts. I get it. Either Ames and I both get in, or neither of us does. Is that it?"

Andy sighed. "You're asking me something no human can know. But yes, that's pretty much my understanding of how Jesus stands our picture of things on its head."

"Ok my oldest, best friend, I probably can't stop thinking the guy was the rottenest prick in the western hemisphere and you were an asshole to have him for a friend. But the thing is, you showed up in my life, right near the end in a way I never could have imagined. I don't much go for these spooky ideas about people showing up just at the right time, but I am knocked back by finding you again. And while it kills me to admit, I think you know a shit load more than I do about how the big guy works.

"This is going to sound like an adolescent girl speaking, but I actually think having you for a friend counts for more with me than even the pleasure I get from thinking Ames will spend eternity slowly frying his sorry ass in hell. Which is just what would happen if I were God."

Andy expelled a long, slow breath. They laughed. "So many things would be very much different if I were God," he said. "Lucky thing for most of the world that I'm not."

"Now," Max said, looking into Andy's eyes, "since you just did it for that Judas, how about giving me absolution, my oldest friend, the priest?"

~~~

XXIX

"OK, now that we've got that God thing figured out," Max said as Andy steered the car through the first big curve on the grade, heading for the San Diego airport, "maybe it's safe for us to do the down and dirty between us. Leave God in heaven. While we're both looking straight ahead instead of facing each other. When Sandra and I have something hard to talk about we do better when we're driving than when we're sitting across from each other.

"So Aldrich Ames doesn't fry forever in hell. I still want to know how you ever let yourself get sucked into being such a close friend of that prick."

Andy was grateful not to be able to see Max's expression. He'd dreaded this, but he knew it had to come.

"Well," Andy began, speaking slowly, "I'd love to tell you it was because clergy have so few friends and are pathetically grateful to those who put themselves forward, especially if they come to church with their wallets open, which he did. What I mean is, I would prefer to tell you that he seduced me and I was weak enough to let him.

"But the truth is I really liked the guy. He was smart, articulate, a really good squash player, had several sweet, good looking wives and did a ton of heavy lifting for our parish.

"Maybe what cinched the deal was that Alice really liked him and liked the two wives we knew. There just weren't that many couples that we both liked equally. Having a social life as a priest was pretty lean pickings."

Andy stopped talking, concentrated on the hairpin turns. Max waited a while before responding.

"I can see all that," he said. "But I picked him off as a phony the moment I met him. You must be a pretty good judge of people. He was a womanizer, a fatal flaw in a spy. I was sure the Agency would send him packing after his internship. But his father had been with the Agency on the administrative side and frankly, the candidates for the clandestine side was pretty lean then, thanks in no small part to you anti-war guys.

"Were you always aware he was undercover for the Agency?"

"No," Andy admitted. "Until about a year before he was caught I bought his identity as an executive with Sears World Trade. One afternoon after squash we were having a few beers. I mentioned something about Sears stock and he struggled to explain. But it was clear he wasn't up to speed with something I knew would be a big deal with anyone who really worked for the company.

"When I pressed him about it, he told me that he was on the Sears payroll, but most of his work was off their books. He said he wasn't at liberty to tell me any more than that.

"I'd put in a few years in a parish in D.C. I knew what that meant. But I never pushed him about it."

They were beyond the switchbacks. As the road straightened out, Andy stole a look at Max.

Good spy, your expression betrays nothing about what you're feeling.

"What about the womanizing part?" Max asked. "You must have been aware of that."

"That's an uncomfortable question, Max. Yes, I knew about that. But not only did I not hold that against him, I kind of admired, oh shit, even envied him. Those were the days of free love, remember? And I wasn't the only randy young priest who convinced himself that sport fucking was a part of the freedom Jesus sponsored, that uptight western culture had shut down. There were lots of rumors floating around in the first century that Christian meetings were really orgies. Some clergy had a run at trying that out.

"Good Lord, Andy, you must have had some crazy parish weekends."

Andy laughed. "Like so much of what was pretty exciting about those days, we were out of our depth, out of control. In fact control was considered a bad word. I'm old enough now to be grateful for having been on the margins of that excess. I'm even more grateful it didn't totally take me down.

It was a lot of fun, exciting. The way lion hunting with bare hands must be."

Max shook his head. "And to think we stiffs in the Agency not only missed out on all that but risked our necks to make it possible for you hedonists to break all the old rules."

Andy shuddered. "That stings. I'm not going to try to make a case for all the excesses, but I could make the case that you in the Agency and the grunts in Vietnam were fighting for some of the same things we were fighting for in the anti-war, free-love movement. Freedom."

That doesn't sound as convincing as it did in those days.

"Get real, Andy. I don't begrudge you the free sex, but it's more than a stretch to compare hippies to those who did combat."

"Is it?" Andy challenged. "Why exactly did you do what you did?"

"You go first," Max responded. "What about burning the flag and free fucking is like fighting for your country?"

"You just said it, Max. Free. So maybe you think hippies were jerks, and maybe they—we—were. But because we're lucky enough to live in this country we were free to be jerks. There were plenty of people who wanted to shut the whole thing down, and sometimes came pretty close in places like the Democratic Convention in 1968. It was a scary time and many of us believed we were testing the promises we've been making and breaking in this country since the beginning."

"A lot of what you say appeals," Max admitted. "But it just doesn't square with the real world. The stuff we were doing was where the rubber meets the road, not highfaluting ideas about how many angels can dance on the head of a pin. Our goal was the make sure our angel was the last one left standing."

"Great line, Max. Probably sums up most Americans' theology."

"I'll tell you one thing," Max said, "I never for one moment believed I was risking my neck so you could get laid."

"I meant to thank you," Andy said. Both laughed.

"We're pretty far afield from the Rick Ames thing," Andy said. "The odd thing is that despite his sexual escapades his so-called morals were more like yours than like mine. He voted for Barry Goldwater. He was the only real conservative friend I had then. One reason I valued his friendship was because I got tired of my politically correct liberal friends. Rick actually thought about things. I almost never agreed with him but I loved trading ideas with him."

Max scowled. "Needing a friend to balance your lame liberalism seems like a pretty weak reason to make someone a close friend, Andy, if you don't mind my saying so."

"As a matter of fact," Andy bristled, "I do mind your saying so. I get why you hate hearing anything good about him, but we're both grown up enough to know no one's all good or all bad, don't you think?"

Max looked out the window to the changing landscape, low to high desert. "Speak for yourself, Reverend Wishy-Washy," he said bitterly. "Sometimes you just have to say someone's evil. The pity of our justice system is that it insists on treating someone like Ames as if he was a citizen who still had rights. If I were in charge he would have been stood up against a wall and shot the day he was caught."

Andy sighed. "I'm not defending Rick Ames, Max. He made me doubt my judgment about people more than anyone I can remember. It infuriates me, not as much as I know it does you, that he did such violence to your agents, caused them to be executed. I'm generally against capital punishment but I might make an exception for him.

"But if there is any integrity to how I have spent my entire adult life, it means no one is totally evil, beyond redemption. And no one, except maybe you, Max, is totally good," Andy said, hoping Max wouldn't take offense at his sarcasm.

"I think that's what atheists believe," Andy said, "that even God isn't powerful enough to set everything right in the end. That there must be a god of evil who is even more powerful than the god of love. There's a religion that believes that, Max, it's Manichaean. But it's not Christian. "

"If you're saying the Christian God loves those guys who flew the planes into the buildings on 9-11," Max's voice was back to steely accusatory. "Then I say your god's an asshole. I'm going to look around for one of those Mani whatchama-callit churches."

Weary, discouraged, Andy had a flashback to a piece he'd seen in something he read the night before he picked up Max at the airport.

An article by a Jungian analyst.

...one should not underestimate the courage it takes to heal from a human betrayal. Betrayal invariably affects the psyche to its deepest roots. When it is made conscious, it is experienced as a threat to one's own being, and the path toward healing is paved with pain.

"You know something Max, I don't honestly think any of us could stand to consciously live with the God I believe in. I throw a hissy fit when I find out that Alice has revealed to one of her women friends that I have a bad temper. If I can't stand Alice telling her friends I'm not perfect, how do I live with God, from whom no secrets are hid?

"I choose to believe God forgives Aldrich Ames, and even those pricks who flew those planes. But I no longer try to pretend to myself that I think that's OK with me. That I can make sense of it. Or even sometimes bear it.

"I hope you won't end up hating me for having been a friend of Aldrich Ames, but I doubt I'll ever forgive myself for it. That's really the point. God, at least the God I have been preaching, not only does stuff we can't—like forgiving people we consider unforgivable—but somehow gets inside us and tears loose things we consider non-negotiable."

"Such as?" Max asked, smoke coming from his mouth and nose.

"Such as patriotism. If God is God, then passionate attachment to one's country takes a back seat to loyalty to the Kingdom."

"And where is this Kingdom that requires greater loyalty than my loyalty to the country that saved my life?" Max bit off his words.

"I don't fucking know," Andy admitted. "The best I can come up with is what Jesus' said when the Pharisees asked him that question. 'The Kingdom is within you.'"

"Next to my gallbladder, maybe," Max said, "which, by the way, got removed a few years ago."

"Look, Max, I don't have answers to this stuff. I don't think anyone does. I have the most impractical understanding of what it means to be a God person. I can't do it myself and I don't even think I would if I could. But that doesn't change anything about what I really think is true. Maybe it was one of the things that finally made me want to stop standing in a pulpit, high above the heads of people, preaching as if I actually understood God or Jesus. I often hated myself for not being able to live what I preached."

"Jesus, Andy, your job ramped up more anxiety in you than mine did."

"I'm not looking for sympathy," Andy said. "It's the monkey on my back that's been riding me ever since that day freshman year in college when I discovered I like getting in the mix with people in trouble."

"So why didn't you become a social worker?" Max asked.

"Because… Look, Max, you're pushing me into a dark corner. I thought God, or what I believed was God, was somehow tapping me on the shoulder when that drunk guy came looking for me. I thought God was saying, 'I've got work for you.'"

"Guess that's what they mean by vocation," Max said.

"Yeah, either that or schizophrenia. It gets dicey as you learn what the Bible really is. Then you do therapy and discover how susceptible you are to wanting to be holy and wonderful.

"All the shit that fundamentalists trot out to prove their bona fides makes me want to vomit. But the truth is, despite all the layers of sophistication I've piled on in the past 60 years, I still feel like my life belongs to God in some way.

"And I can't live up to it."

Andy choked back a sob. Max looked away, stunned, embarrassed for his friend. He put his hand lightly on Andy's shoulder.

"This isn't all just to get me to be OK with you and Ames, right?" Max asked.

Andy's tears gave way to laughter. He concentrated, the traffic increasing as they got closer to San Diego. "Oh shit, Max, I wish it was that simple. I do want you to be OK about me and Ames, but this is about so much more.

"I've never said this to another living soul and if you ever tell anyone I said it I will call you a liar. What the fuck did I think I was doing getting myself ordained a priest? I don't know if there's a god, I don't know if I think Jesus was a real person, I don't see anything that makes me think there's more after you die. I don't know shit."

Andy felt like a deflated balloon. He evaded Max's eyes, now fixed on him. Neither of them spoke. Finally Andy broke the silence.

"I'm so sorry, Max. You didn't ask for that. I don't know what ever possessed me to say all that."

"You want to know something really weird, Andy? When you just spouted all that out of your mouth, I had this really clear sense that I understood for the first time why I was so good at turning agents.

"I must secrete some pheromone that makes people tell me things they have sworn never to tell anyone. It stood me in pretty good stead with the Agency, but as you might imagine, it can be a pretty heavy burden, listening to shit I never expected or dreamed they would tell me.

"You poor guy. Preaching when you weren't sure yourself must have made for a tortured existence as a parish priest."

"Maybe that's the worst part," Andy said, his composure returning. "I didn't. I loved it. And I daresay I was pretty good at it. I'm not even sure what haunts me, except my contempt for some colleagues who so clearly were fakers."

"Were you a faker, Andy?"

"Sometimes, when I couldn't bear to take away hope from someone who was hanging by a thread, and I was afraid the thread was about to break. But no. I suppose there must be plenty of priests who buy the whole package. Not the ones I got close to—of course those would be guys like me. We had to dance around a lot of the old orthodoxy."

"You mean Mary wasn't really a virgin?" Max belly laughed.

"Oh man," Andy said, finally able to laugh a little himself. "That's an easy one. The real buggers are about prayer and a god who decides, like Santa Claus, who's good and bad, who's going to get candy and who gets a bundle of switches.

"Not to mention the contemporary version of indulgences. Who gives the most money to the church and gets to pose as Saint Rockefeller."

"What about the doctrine of just war?" Max asked. "Do you think war can be justified under certain conditions?"

"The thing is, Max, it seems just incredibly cheeky for me to say whether some war is justified. I admire the Roman Catholics working so hard to come to terms with that. But I don't buy it. Am I a pacifist? No, I don't have the discipline or courage. A friend was outraged when he read that Gandhi not only befriended Hitler, but after the Holocaust was revealed he said the Jews should have gone willingly rather than resist so futilely. Gandhi was being consistent. Like the Roman Catholics about birth control and abortion.

"I just can't ever be consistent about God and us. Nothing about the real world strikes me as consistent. That's trying to make God have a human mind." Andy sighed.

"Try preaching that," he said.

Andy took a right off the highway, headed for the airport. They were early for Max's flight. Andy drove into the cell phone waiting lot, parked and turned off the motor.

"We've got just a couple of minutes before I need to drop you," he said. "And I'm hoping we might reach some place where we're both comfortable with Ames and the differences in how we see things before you leave.

"Speaking for myself, I feel our bond of friendship may be stronger than ever. But I can't deny there are some pretty big differences between us, and I'm not sure if my friendship with Aldrich Ames is the biggest of them."

Max stretched his legs, pushed his aching back against the seat. "I've never had a friend I talked with like this, at least not since I was a grownup," he said.

"If you had told me the kinds of things we'd be talking about, I probably would have said no thanks. I sure didn't expect to find out that I may be a bigger believer than you. But I have to say, Andy, hanging with you is pretty rich.

"The Ames part has me stymied, not so much because he was your friend—there's no accounting for how we choose friends—but because I don't know yet whether I can let go of how angry it makes me just to think of that rat shit sitting at your table, playing godfather to your daughter. I should admit to you that Sandra briefly thought he was pretty cool until I set her straight about what a con artist he was.

"Anyway, look, don't let it go to your head that I don't have any other friends like you. Or maybe any other friends at all. But I do consider you my dear friend, almost like a brother.

"I wonder if we hadn't missed those 50 years, if we'd have made this connection?

"One thing for sure, you're not like any priest I ever knew."

"And you're not like any spy I ever knew," Andy said. "I suppose neither of us should expect to live a whole lot longer, but I hope there might be time enough to see where this goes."

He started the car and backed out of the parking place.

"No need to get out of the car when you leave me off," Max said. "We may be just this side of gay lovers, but I'm not into hugging good byes."

Andy laughed. "Fair enough. Hugging is obligatory in the church business and it gets to be thin gruel after a while. Hugging people because it's in the script even if you really don't want to."

Andy pulled up to the curb, put out his hand, and the two of them shook. Max stepped out of the car, opened the back door to retrieve his suitcase. He leaned down to look at Andy.

"In the spy business, a hug was considered putting yourself at risk for a shiv in the ribs. See you, amigo, it's been real." Max turned toward the terminal.

Andy watched until he disappeared into the terminal. *That's a big limp, you've got there, old friend.* As he pulled into traffic his mind wandered to Max's admission that Sandra had once admired Aldrich Ames. *One thing to discover your friend was a friend of your enemy, but how about your wife?*

~~~

XXX

Reset

"How'd it go?" Alice asked Andy.

"Well, in many ways it was great, in some, less so. I'm spent. Feel like I ran a marathon. Maybe a bowl of soup and then off to bed. Be ready to talk at breakfast..

He slept soundly until 1 A.M., then tossed for an hour, unable to find a comfortable position.

I can't believe I told Max that stuff about my latent agnosticism. It seemed to piss him off even more than the Aldrich Ames thing. Or maybe it scared me more. After 50 years you might think I'd have made peace with it. Maybe I would have if I knew what I really believe. Oh, for God's sake, man, give yourself a break. You were a good priest. That you can still be honest about your agnosticism means you didn't lose your nerve and sell out.

~

Though he usually couldn't sleep on planes, Max slept most of the flight to Charlottesville where Sandra met him. He climbed into the passenger seat, slumped down and sighed.

"Big sigh," Sandra said, "strenuous trip?"

Max looked straight ahead. "No, I wouldn't call it strenuous. At least not physically. But it was unlike any time I've spent with anyone, maybe since Andy and I were kids."

Before she pulled away from the curb Sandra gave him a long look. She touched his cheek in an unusual display of affection between these two tough old spies. "You look spent. Was it OK?"

Max took a moment to respond. "Well, yes, I have to say it was better than OK, it was pretty great. But I still don't know what to make of it all. Some stuff we got into was surreal."

"You mean the Aldrich Ames stuff?" she asked as she put the car in gear. Her voice betrayed uneasiness.

"We did get into that and we both got predictably testy. I think there's more if we decide to do more. But that didn't get to me as much as Andy's letting me see a pretty real piece of his insides, the stuff I guess we all have in us somewhere but are terrified of letting someone see. I think he was looking for me to do the same. In a way I did I think, but maybe because he's a priest and does lots of therapy he knows a lot more about his insides than I think I do. Probably more than I want to, which may be a problem for Andy, though it didn't seem to be."

"Oh Max," Sandra said, putting her hand on his knee while keeping her eye on the road. "You always think everyone else is better than you at everything. You may be good at hiding as a spy but you're the most self-aware, honest guy I know. Especially among your colleagues at the Agency."

"Thanks. I'm beat. Traveling sucks these days." He looked out the window, grateful for the familiar view across the valley to the mountains. Soon his head flopped onto his chest. He didn't wake until Sandra was guiding the car through the narrow turns on the rough road that lead to their house.

"I made some curry, just need to heat it up," she said as Max wheeled his suitcase into the house behind her.

"Great," he answered. "I have just about enough energy left to swallow. Then I'm headed for the sack."

~~~

XXXI

From: andy@gmail.com
To: maxman@comcast.net
Subject: Still friends?

Hope you don't mind carrying on for a while through this medium, Max. I hate the phone. I'm already thinking about how to do another face-to-face meeting while we both still have most of our marbles.

I expected the business about Ames to be the toughest thing we'd have to deal with but unless I missed some signals from you, it wasn't. I still expect we have some unfinished issues. I feel much better about that than I did before that visit. If that required extra effort from you I appreciate it.

The picture people have of me often surprises me, especially people I feel close to. I find myself having to keep from apologizing for not believing in God exactly as you do. As I said, I have a fierce sense of the holy, just not one that fits very neatly into how it seems most people think about God.

I catch myself wanting to justify my being a parish priest all those years. I'm always concerned about not meeting the expectations you and others may have about what that required of me.

I feel more passionately now than when I began, that I have been following what the church calls the Holy Spirit. I might be more comfortable referring to it as conviction, or maybe even desire, only because it seems presumptuous to me to claim even modest certainty about hearing or understanding God's intentions.

But every time I looked out at a congregation, or stood by the bed of a dying person, or listened to a despairing couple talk about a divorce, some kind of empathy welled up in me that made me love those people.

If I believe nothing else about God it is that there is nothing in heaven or on earth that can separate us from God's love for us. I don't know exactly what I mean by that. It's what brings us here from nothing in the first place, and it's hard as hell to experience because everything in our culture teaches us we aren't worthy of being loved like that. I know because that's the issue I struggle with personally.

Even though it makes me crazy sometimes I believe what you and I are about to do—die—doesn't separate us from God's love. If we have long enough maybe I'll get a chance to talk about why I suspect dying is ecstasy.

Maybe for you that doesn't seem enough for me to presume to call myself a priest of God. But it finally has come to seem not merely enough for me, but the rock on which my identity as a priest rests.

Just needed to get that off my chest so I could hold my head up with you.

So grateful for our reconnection, Max.

Andy

From: **maxman@comcast.net**
To: **andy@gmail.com**
Subject: Friends Forever

Thanks for that Andy. In all honesty, no, that doesn't seem enough for someone to let themselves be ordained. But that only means it wouldn't be enough for me if I was considering it. But your passion convinces me that however it got translated into you, your vocation is real. Just hard for me to get, exactly.

I'm hoping you're right about dying, though I can't make heads or tails out of what you wrote.

It's hardly comparable but when people find out I'm a spy they have a shitload of ideas about what that must mean about me. And just about all of them are wrong. I think I became a spy in some way kind of like you became a priest. I had to. I knew I needed to do something to repay my country for saving me. And because of the way I'm strung together I knew it was going to have to be hard. And, preferably, dangerous.

I intended to join the Marines, until that CIA guy knocked on my dorm room door that day. I'm not especially brave. I do everything I can to avoid pain. Can't stand most of the pretentious assholes who show up for interviews with the clandestine service brimming over with false bravado.

But the idea of persuading (seducing) a Soviet agent, giving him a taste of life in care of the good old USA, was such a turn on I couldn't resist.

Maybe I'm some sort of pervert, but that's never lost its hold on me.

So it's not so much that I can't imagine having the balls to become a priest unless I bought the whole package—which I couldn't. I actually kind of get what you're saying because I don't think I was much like most of the other guys in the agency. I appreciate your letting me see the guts of your vocation. It moves me, a lot. Now I've tried to give you a look at mine.

Friends forever, hooked together by our weird take on our peculiar jobs.

~~~

XXXII

Another Penny Drops

Andy played the North Course at Torrey Pines two weeks later with three friends he enjoyed, except during election years when their politics could give him a sour stomach.

Over hamburgers at the grill afterward Andy let himself get sucked into conversation about the primaries, something he promised himself he wouldn't let happen.

"So. What do you make of Donald Trump getting one landslide victory after another?" asked Doug Lancaster, a real estate broker who'd broken the multi-million dollar sales record the previous year.

Andy knew he was being baited, but the smug expression on Doug's face touched a raw nerve.

"I think what every sensible person thinks," he said, already aware he was headed for deep water, "that the man is a sick joke."

"Don't you think that's a little arrogant?" Doug suggested. "Ten million people have voted for him so far and you think he's a joke? So I guess that makes your judgment superior to those 10 million."

Andy could feel the blood rushing to his face. He knew Doug was loving seeing him squirm.

"Let's not pretend those votes are representative of anything more than unfocused anger," he said, hearing himself bite off his words. "Trump is a demagogue who has found a way to use his celebrity to exploit people who are feeling screwed."

"You know, Andy, I always thought you were a good priest, but your liberal views really could get in the way. You were ordained to talk about Jesus, not that slimy Barack Obama."

"You know, Doug, it's one thing to disagree with President Obama, but calling him slimy is more of that nasty racist stuff that people like you have been using to poison the waters of this country ever since he was elected."

The other two golfers busied themselves dressing their hamburgers with condiments, avoiding eye contact.

Doug leaned across the table, his eyes narrowed. "You dare call me a racist? You and your do-gooder, holier-than-thou liberalism doesn't cut it with me.

"You set yourself up as the sweet forgiving Jesus when Aldrich Ames was found out. We all know the real reason you stood up for him. Everyone knows Alice had a fling with him."

One of the other two put his hand on Doug's arm. "Easy Doug, we're here for some Saturday fun. No need to make this a federal case."

Doug shook off his hand. "I'm sick of Andy posing as some pious saint when all he's doing is spreading liberal bull-shit. And covering for his wife in the Ames thing is pathetic."

Andy suddenly stood up, nearly knocking over the table. "You've crossed the line, Doug, making up shit like that just to piss me off. When you're ready to apologize, we can talk again."

Andy turned and walked out of the grill. He concentrated on keeping his back straight. It took all his strength not to let his wobbly legs give way. On the drive home he chastised himself for letting Doug lure him into that trap.

What an asshole, he thought, though he wasn't sure whether he meant Doug or himself. *Pulling Alice into the argument, using her to try to win a political point. Doug can be unprincipled but that takes the fucking cake. Watch your driving, man. Your blood pressure must be off the chart.*

By the time he pulled into the driveway Andy had calmed down. *Doug must be really desperate, having that nutcase looking like he might be the nominee. Even Doug wouldn't normally stoop so low as to try to drag Alice into it.*

He went into the house. Alice was in the pantry arranging flowers for the mantle. She looked up as he came in, smiled. "How was your golf? Make a hole in one today?"

Andy laughed. "That'll be the day, a hole in one on the North course. Even Tiger hasn't managed that. I played up to my usual duffer game. Almost forgotten about the golf, got into a real row afterward with Doug."

Alice turned away from arranging flowers. "Oh, Andy, you didn't let him get to you. You know how he loves to get your goat. I can't believe you gave him the chance."

"He referred to Obama as slimy; I lost it, called him a racist."

She took a step toward him, put her hand on his shoulder. "Well, he is, but I don't think he's even aware of it. That must have really set him off."

"Oh, you have no idea," Andy said. "I ended getting up and leaving."

"You've got to be kidding," she said. "You actually walked out and left him sitting there?"

"Yep, and I'd do it again. Just realized I left him to pay the check. Now I'm doubly happy I walked out."

"I can't imagine what he could have said to make you do that. The one thing you always say is, never leave until the matter is resolved."

"Well, I did and I'm not sorry, that miserable prick."

"Andy, I never see you like this, what in the world did he say?"

"Never mind, Alice, it doesn't bear repeating."

"You wouldn't believe how red your face is," Alice said, drying her hands on her apron and pulling him into an embrace. "Come have a seat in the kitchen. I'll fix you a cup of tea. I didn't think you could get this angry at anyone except me."

Andy released some of the tension in his shoulders and settled into Alice's embrace. "I'll take you up on that cup of tea. I can get pretty mad at you, but nothing like how mad I got at Doug."

"Andy!" She took a step back, looked into his eyes, and said, "This just isn't like you. Are you OK?"

"Oh I'm OK, just pissed to beat the band."

Alice led him into the kitchen. She put the kettle on the stove and motioned to Andy to sit down. He dropped heavily into the chair, head down, eyes focused on his feet.

"Andy, what in the world did he say?"

"Doesn't matter. Just a big lie he made up to goad me. And I'm ashamed to say he succeeded."

"What sort of a lie?"

"Look, Alice, the last thing I want is to carry this any further."

"Carry what further?" Alice probed, now feeling anxious about she didn't know what.

"Don't push me, Alice, it's not worth it."

"Andy, it sure is worth it for you to completely let yourself lose it like this. I think we need to talk about whatever it was." She turned back to the stove as the kettle began to whistle.

"He said something terrible about you," Andy said, his voice nearly inaudible. Alice wasn't sure she understood what he said.

Alice pivoted from the stove toward Andy. "Did you say he said something about me?"

Andy nodded without looking up at her.

"Like what?"

"Stupid," Andy muttered. "Really pissed me off."

"Like what?" she pressed.

"He picked on what he knew was a sore spot, about Rick."

"What about Rick?" Alice asked warily.

"He suggested you had a thing with him." Now Andy could barely hear his own words.

"A thing Andy, you mean an affair?"

"He called it a fling."

"But sexual, right?" she asked, hearing her own shaky voice. "Doug said I had an affair with Rick?"

"Yes. Lucky for him I didn't paste him in the mouth, right there in the grill."

Ominous silence.

"No wonder you're so upset.

"You know, Andy, I'd never set out to do anything to hurt you."

He felt an ominous chill. "Of course."

"I once came dangerously close to having an affair with Aldrich." Alice turned from the stove toward Andy, looking at him. Andy didn't look back.

"What do you mean, exactly?" he asked.

Alice sat in the chair opposite Andy. She leaned forward, putting her hands on his knees. "When you were in that fight with the vestry about whether to take a piece of the ad in the paper opposing the Vietnam War, and Rick was Senior Warden, there was a moment when he told me he would support you no matter what, and that it wasn't because he agreed with you, but because he cared about me. And I fell for it."

"Fell for what?"

"For somebody who understood what your principled stand cost me."

"And the price was betraying me in an affair with Aldrich?"

"Nearly," Alice admitted, removing her hands from his knees. She sat back in her chair and watched Andy's expression. She couldn't read it. "I had no idea I was so wounded, so vulnerable. But I was."

"You said 'nearly.' How near?"

"I backed out before anything happened that could technically be called an affair. But I'm not going to try to tell you I didn't betray our love because in that moment I did. I felt like you stopped caring about me, only cared about winning that fight. Rick sensed that and offered me solace."

"That prick! Max was so right about him. My supposed best friend, senior warden, the fucking fox in the henhouse. He was a traitor to more than the country.

"But you! Oh God, Alice, I never imagined this."

Alice began to cry. "Oh Andy believe me, neither did I. I would give anything for it never to have happened. I never stopped loving you, but I have had awful moments when I felt like I was more a convenience than your beloved wife. Sometimes I felt like you needed to have me by your side, but your real love was serving your righteous God. That's no excuse, I know, and I don't mean it as one. It was just..." Her sobbing interrupted her speaking.

"Oh Jesus," Andy said. He pulled his chair closer, putting his hands on her knees. "I don't know if I even believe in God. Your love is the most of God I ever expect to know. And I threw it into the toilet. I let you hang out there while

I played moral hero. Oh Alice, I don't know why you didn't fuck everyone in the church.

"I'm so sorry," he said. His tears now came in a flood. His shoulders were heaving.

Alice looked up. They were finally face to face. "You don't have anything to apologize for," she said. "You didn't betray me. You were just doing your job, obeying your conscience."

Andy stood up and began pacing back and forth. "That's where you're wrong, Alice. Maybe I didn't have actual affairs, but I let so many women believe I loved them, that I understood them in ways their husbands didn't. And I got off on their fawning over me. That was a betrayal of you as much as the one near miss with that asshole Ames."

"Oh Andy," she said, her tears began again. "I wish I could believe that. I thought you'd hate me as much as I hate myself for letting myself get into that."

"Alice, I probably don't really believe everything I've ever said about God and Jesus, but one thing I believe more than I believe I'm standing here, is that once you are loved the way you have loved me and I have tried to love you, nothing can undo that. And I mean nothing. Certainly not a completely understandable moment with a master manipulator like Aldrich Ames, when your pseudo hero husband has hung you out to dry."

Alice's tears turned to wracking sobs. She choked and her shoulders shook. Andy walked behind her and began massaging her shoulders.

Her crying slackened enough for her to speak. "I've heard you say those things to parishioners who've done horrible things. It's your job and you're good at it, but I'm your wife and I can't make myself believe you forgive me."

"Alice, Alice, you're right about one thing; I'm devastated. This does violence to everything I've always believed about you and me. I probably can't forgive you all the way, not yet. I want to kill Ames.

"But it's not about whether we forgive, or even about what happened with Rick. It's about whether all the stupid shit we do—and we do a lot of shit, all of us—gets the last word.

"And the answer is no. If there is any such thing as God, God gets the last word. Which is why you and I are still married after all these years. God knows we've given each other plenty of reasons to bail. And this one isn't the worst."

Alice's crying had stopped. She looked up at Andy quizzically, as if he'd said something she'd never heard before.

"I've never admitted this to anyone," she said, "but there have been times when I wanted to kill you. And times when I would have happily killed your whole stupid congregation. I swallowed all that because it seemed like it was about what was wrong with me, that I couldn't see how holy you were, and how much the congregation needed and deserved every ounce of you.

"You remember when we went to Bishop Arnold before we were married and he asked me how I would feel about being married to God? I laughed, blew him off, said I wasn't interested in being married to God, or competing with God for your attention.

"But you know what, Andy?" Tears again. "I wish I could stop believing in God, instead of hating God for claiming so much of you I wanted."

Andy's tears began again. He came around from behind Alice, sat in the chair opposite her, leaning forward.

"I wish I could blame that on God," he said through his tears. "I don't know anything about God. Really, I don't. But if there is any such thing as God that even remotely resembles what I preach about that god doesn't give a shit what I think about him. What God has given me in answer to my fumbling prayer is you, Alice.

"It's totally beyond human ability to take two stubborn, edgy people like us and make a 52-year marriage. Can't be done. But here we are. If I need more than that for my creed, there's only idolatry.

"It doesn't get more real than this.

"So fuck Aldrich Ames. Or don't fuck him. It doesn't matter."

Their crying mixed with laughter.

~~~

XXXII

That wasn't the end of their come-to-Jesus moment. Andy prized himself on being able to forgive, to let go of hurts. But he knew sometimes the outward show covered what went on inside him.

Aldrich fucking Ames, I can't believe it. I must have been so preoccupied, or was it that I didn't want to see? What would I have done had I known at the time? I have no idea.

For years Alice had lived in dread of Andy knowing. She tried to comfort herself that she and Rick never had an actual sexual affair but she understood the betrayal of her heart.

I still can't believe I let myself do that. Lame that I rationalized how lonely I was, feeling abandoned by Andy who was surrounding himself with parish sycophants.

"You want to know something, Andy," she said over breakfast the next morning. "I really hated watching you let yourself be seduced by those assholes who fawned over you."

Andy went on alert. "Is this going to be trying to justify to me how you got involved with Rick, Alice? Because you don't need to explain it. I don't blame you for getting pissed about people lionizing me. Fact is, now that I have some distance, I am plenty embarrassed about it myself that I was so needy."

Alice put her spoon down hard enough to let them both know she was angry. "Goddamn it Andy! Would you stop being the noble offended husband. In fact that's not where I was heading with this.

"What I wanted to say—and yes, it is triggered by the thing about Rick—is how often I pretended to be the dutiful rector's wife while I was overflowing with resentment. And I hated myself for that because it ended up with me turning my resentment into contempt for you. But I did, Andy. I got sick to my stomach watching you charm and cajole people who were manipulating you for their own purposes, and who I knew full well you wanted to throttle."

They stared across the table at each other, neither speaking. Andy held a spoonful of granola halfway to his mouth, as if in a film that had suddenly frozen. He put the spoon back into the bowl.

"I'm having a hard time figuring out whether I'm more angry or sad," he said, his gaze fixed on her. "I don't feel like apologizing for those years we spent while I was a parish priest. But I know there was a hell of a lot about it that required more of each of us than we probably could manage. Maybe it's naïve and self-serving of me to think we signed on for this together. I know I pretended to be a nicer person than I really am a lot of the time. But it's not as if we tried to fool each other, even if we were fooling parishioners."

Alice's crying became louder. She shook her head. "No, no, Andy, we weren't fooling each other; we were each fooling ourselves, pretending that if only we were nice enough everything would turn out OK.

"You want to know what really attracted me to Rick? It wasn't his smoothness, or even his being so sympathetic to me when he sensed I was feeling neglected. Oh no, it was the outlaw in him, the steeliness that he tried to keep people from seeing. I sensed it in him right from the start. And after trying so hard to be a good rector's wife I found his dark side exciting, real.

"The rest of the world may have been shocked when he was arrested but I wasn't."

Andy stared at her, wide-eyed. "Jesus Christ, Alice, was I that boring that you went looking to fuck a criminal?"

Alice slammed her open hand down on the table, making the dishes rattle. "God damn it, Andy. I didn't fuck Rick Ames, even though I may have wanted to once. And the reason I didn't was because of my caring for you and for our marriage. Yes, you could be a boring predictable asshole, even nice to a fault.

"Look, let's be real here; I don't know whether you ever went over the line with one of those women who fawned over you, and I don't want to know. I really don't. But we're not the only well married couple who have looked for a little more sexual excitement than any marriage over five years can provide.

"If Rick Ames has done nothing else good in his life, maybe his making us open up about some of the shit we've buried all these years is enough to get him off for good behavior."

Alice laughed. Andy laughed.

"Good God Alice, this isn't how I pictured our golden years. You've heard me say a thousand times how much better it is to get it all out on the table. But I meant for other couples, not us."

Their laughter turned to stomach-crunching guffaws.

When Andy finally caught his breath, he said, "I always wanted to be your hero, Alice. But I never felt like anyone's hero. I believed a lot of what I preached, but I know I swallowed more than was good for me to try to keep peace. With the congregation and with you. I knew you were aware of that, but I guess I'm surprised to learn how angry it made you."

"I don't think angry is the word I'd choose," she said. "Maybe disappointment that you couldn't provide everything I ever wanted. Don't try to tell me you found everything you ever dreamed of in me."

"Well," Andy tried to look thoughtful, as if he were considering it. "Maybe bigger breasts. But then you'd expect me to have a bigger penis."

That seemed to settle the matter, at least for the moment. Then each got up from the table, picked up dishes, carried them into the kitchen.

"I'll do the dishes," Andy said.

"How did I know that was coming?" Alice asked as she kissed him full on the mouth. "Think I'll just curl up on the couch and read the paper." She went into the living room. Andy rolled up his sleeves, put on an apron, and began tending to the dishes.

~~~

XXXIII

From: **andy@gmail.com**
To: **maxman@comcast.net**
Subject: Another round?

You up for one more go round, Max? Time's marching on and I keep having this feeling there's so much more we could explore. I know you don't travel and I don't want to burden you and Sandra again, so if it suits you for me to come round sometime in the next few weeks, how about making me a reservation somewhere nearby for a couple of nights?

From: **maxman@comcast.net**
To: **andy@gmail.com**
Subject: Another round?

I'm up for it, Andy. The docs want to have another go at my back. They won't say it outright but I know it's a tug of war between my becoming bedridden, and dying on the operating table. Not up for the first, and even though I'm not eager for the second, it's an easy choice for me. Just have to find an anesthesiologist who's not scared of a suit if I mort.

That's going to take some time, and I'm sitting around twiddling my thumbs, so this is a good time. I spoke with Sandra, and she suggested that Alice come along. We're all close enough to the pearly gates to have some candid conversation. Sort of looking to close the circle. Too late to rewrite our legacies. I think Sandra's up for making a new friend too. There's a B&B at the foot of our hill, run by friends. Two guest rooms. Simple but clean. You can have breakfast there, then come to us for lunch and light supper. If you agree I will reserve a room for you two for a week from next Wednesday and Thursday nights. Lots to talk about, I'm sure.

~

Andy waited until after dinner that next night to broach the subject with Alice. Andy was facing the sink, rinsing glasses. Alice was putting leftovers into the fridge.

"I emailed Max suggesting another visit. He emailed me back and said he and Sandra would like you to come too."

Alice straightened up, considering Andy's back. "Why now? Seems kind of crazy, adding me to the mix at this late stage. You're not looking to turn me in about the Ames business, I hope."

"They just want to meet you, close the circle Alice. Of course I wouldn't bring up Ames with them.

"They're the kind of people you don't meet often. Max has the largest collection of assault weapons in private hands, anywhere. It's an experience not to be missed."

"Sure hate to miss a chance to sit around with a bunch of deadly weapons. Look, Andy, Max is your friend. I know finding him again has meant a lot to you. But I really don't think I need to get involved."

Andy turned from the sink and faced her. "I'm not going to push you, Alice. I'd love to introduce you to them because I'm so proud to be married to you. I don't have to answer their email right away. Let's sleep on it."

At breakfast the following morning as Andy poured her coffee, Alice put her hand on his waist. "That was an incredibly nice thing you said about wanting to introduce me to Max and Sandra. I'd love to go with you."

From: **andy@gmail.com**
To: **maxman@comcast.net**
Subject: Love to come

Alice and I would love to come next Wednesday and spend two nights at your friends' B&B. There's a flight that gets into Charlottesville around noon, if that works for you.

From: **maxman@comcast.net**
To: **andy@gmail.com**
Subject: Visit

Perfect. Call when you get in and get settled, and Sandra will come fetch you. We'll have the afternoon and evening, then the same again Thursday. Really looking forward to seeing you and meeting Alice.

~

On the flight Alice began to fret. "Do you think it will be obvious to Max and Sandra how nervous I am about meeting them?"

Andy took a sip of his tomato juice before responding. "Why should you be anxious, Alice? Are you worried that the Rick Ames business will somehow come up? I see no reason it should. I really think Max and I have said all there is to say about that."

Alice sighed. "It's the most dicey issue that's come up between you two since you met again. And our own piece of it makes it hard to imagine it would just disappear into thin air now."

"Maybe not, but even if it did, there's absolutely no reason it should include anything about you and Rick. You know, Alice, I wish you could let go of that. It's the only serious near miss you ever had in our marriage. I'm ashamed that I had a lot more, as you know painfully well." He looked at Alice. She had turned toward the window. "At least it's the only one I know about."

Alice turned back toward him, laughing. "Oh, Andy, I almost wish there were others. Not because I'd like to balance your randy history, which still pisses me off when I think about it, but because maybe it would make me a more interesting woman."

Andy laughed. "Alice, if you were any more interesting, I would long ago have been left in your wake. So you didn't do sport fucking. I'm just glad you didn't dump me for my having such an unconscionably long adolescence."

Alice's laugh this time was louder. "It's our little secret Andy. You are a man, which by definition means an endless adolescent. Maybe a lot of your flock didn't see that because they needed you to be a full fledged grownup, but I knew it. I even found a lot of it rather beguiling, at least when it didn't involve your zipper."

"That stung a little," Andy said. "I gave you a compliment and left myself vulnerable. I am grateful you stuck with me, but I wish you didn't have to beat me up about my weaknesses."

Alice put her hand on his knee. "Sorry, dear guy. I meant it more in fun than to beat you up. I guess I'm feeling pretty nervous about meeting your friends. Makes me testy."

Andy kissed her on the cheek. "They're going to love you, Alice. Everyone does."

~~~

XXXIV

Sandra was waiting at the convenience store when they drove up in their rental car. She embraced them both warmly.

As Sandra expertly maneuvered the SUV up the narrow, winding gravel road, Alice expressed her surprise at the condition of the road.

"I wondered why you insisted on driving us to your house rather than our getting there on our own, Sandra. And I appreciate it. Do they ever do anything to improve this road?"

Sandra smiled. "It's a private road. We maintain it. Or rather we don't maintain it. We like that it's hard for anyone to drive up it."

"Anyone else live up here?" Alice asked.

"Just a couple of old retired spies like us. We all did things that didn't endear us to some people. Not that anyone cares or even remembers us any more. Just an old habit, making ourselves as inaccessible as possible. Not like beloved old priests, I guess."

Alice laughed. "You'd be amazed."

Andy rolled his eyes.

"Max has some news from his doc," Sandra said. "I'll let him tell you. Just to say the timing of your visit is really good. Glad you've come."

~

When they walked through the front door, Max called from the living room where he was stretched out in his uphol-stered adjustable chair. "Come greet your oldest friend in the world! Older even than last time you saw me."

Alice stayed in the front hall with Sandra while Andy went in to Max.

"Forgive me for not getting up and showing proper respect for my better," Max said, "but my fucking surgeon turned me down on fixing my back and I'm feeling a little low."

Andy knelt by the chair, awkwardly embracing Max. "Now your better turns out to be no better than you at get-ting up," Andy laughed, as he struggled to get his feet under-neath him. As he took hold of the back of Max's chair to assist his aching knees, the chair twisted around, so it faced away from Andy.

"Jesus, Andy, I appreciate your show of affection, but maybe you'd help turn my chair back so I won't have to look down the barrel of that bazooka."

Andy shifted the chair back. Max saw Alice standing beside Sandra at the edge of the room. He beamed a huge, friendly grin. "Alice," he said, "so you're the one who tamed my oldest friend. I can see why. Andy said a lot of nice things about you, but his description fell far short of how beautiful you are. I suppose the exorbitant priest's salary was what won you over."

Alice smiled. "You're every bit the rascal Andy described, Max. Andy's pretty fussy about who he chooses to consider a friend. You must know that you top the list."

Seeing Max's eyes mist up, Sandra said, "Before we hand out the awards, how about a cup of tea? And if you two are anywhere near the age we are, you must need to visit the bathroom."

Andy led Alice down the hall to the guest room bathroom. When he closed the door, she said, "You didn't tell me he was immobilized."

"He wasn't. He looks way more wasted than when I was here before. That was pretty ominous, what Sandra said about news from his doctor. Turns out the back doctor won't operate. Max was counting on that, even though he knew he might not survive anesthesia."

When they went back to the living room Max had cranked up the back of his chair to a sitting position. Sandra was tending the tea pot from the low table in front of the sofa where she was sitting. She poured four cups. When she handed one to Max he winced with pain as he turned to put it on the table next to his chair. Andy and Alice sat on the sofa on either side of Sandra. After each had taken a first sip, Sandra welcomed them.

"We've been eagerly looking forward to your visit. Life has its way of visiting us with challenges, and having close friends around for them makes a difference."

"What sort of challenges?" Andy asked.

Max smiled. "You know I expected to be going in for more back surgery. I said the hardest part would be finding an anesthesiologist willing to risk putting a chronic smoker with one and a half lungs to sleep, for fear of not being able to wake him up again.

"Well, turns out not only will no anesthesiologist risk his license doing that, but the MRI shows the so-called good lung is loaded with cancer. They wanted to biopsy it but I told them that would be like trying to make a pet of a road-killed skunk." Max's hacking smoker's laugh was the only sound in the room.

"Max," Sandra protested, "that's a little harsh, don't you think?"

"Maybe," Max retorted, "but not as harsh as dying of lung cancer."

Andy broke the uncomfortable silence that followed. "That's terrible news. I couldn't be sorrier. You know, Max, I've always told myself that when I receive a diagnosis like yours, if I'm not lucky enough to drop dead, I'll refuse treatment. But I've always feared I wouldn't have the courage to do that. I might have known you would.

"I admire you for that, dear guy, but it breaks my heart."

"You sky pilots have a way with words, Andy," said Max, "but the fact is it takes more courage than I have to do the really heroic thing and see if I can eke out a little more time. Probably not fair to Sandra, but I've had enough. I'm tired."

"Now Max," Sandra said, "we talked it through; we made this decision together."

"Any idea how long?" Andy asked.

"They won't talk about that," Max answered. "But you can tell by the way they look away and don't talk about follow-up appointments, they don't think it'll be long."

"What's it like now?" Andy asked. "I mean your body as well as your spirit?"

"With a lot of help from Sandra, I've gotten pretty good at staying mostly ahead of the really terrible pain. By just about any measure I guess you'd have to call me a junkie. Luckily my doc doesn't seem uneasy about my taking these huge doses. It's about all I can do to get to the bathroom, and into bed at night."

"We've thought about how to manage when Max really can't get around at all," Sandra said. "We have a good younger friend, thank God, who does skilled nursing. She said she and a woman she works with will come."

"Look," Max interrupted, "we've got enough morphine in this house to bring down a squad of Special Forces. I don't intend to linger. And I'm not interested in having potty patrol in charge of me."

"And your spirits?" Andy repeated.

"Come on, preacher man," Max said, "you're talking to a spy. I spent my entire adult life preparing myself to die.

I always thought it would be more exciting than this, but then I never imagined living this long. But spirits? I don't do spirits."

"Bullshit," Sandra injected. "Andy's your oldest, best, maybe only friend. You can drop your façade. He won't betray you to the Agency."

"I don't think I need to explain to Andy that a death sentence isn't exactly a great way to start a day," Max said. "He's a priest, been through this with lots of people. Maybe we can save playing taps for another time. Right now I've got my oldest best friend who also happens to be a priest. Even a guy with two good lungs would be happy about that. I'm not feeling sorry for myself and I would be grateful if none of you tried to change that.

"I could still use some lunch."

Their laughter was too high-pitched, forced. An awkward silence followed, finally broken by Sandra.

"OK everyone, I've made Max's favorite chili. What say we go the table and have some lunch? Corn bread too. Andy, if you'll help Max get out of that chair—there's a button on the arm that makes the back push him forward—just be careful not to eject him into that bayonet on the wall. Alice, maybe you'd help me pour iced tea."

The four friends ate their chili in silence. None of them looked up as they spooned it to their mouths.

When she had finished her bowl, Alice, feeling overwhelmed by Max's news, turned to Sandra. "I've only just met you, Sandra, but I feel as close to you in this moment as I do to anyone I'd call a dear friend. My heart aches for you both." Her eyes filled

"That means more than maybe you can know," Sandra responded. "We're pretty isolated up on this mountain. Not that we're not used to it. Spies don't get to have a lot of social life, and frankly, neither of us ever cared for it. But I have to admit it can feel pretty bleak sometimes. When Max and Andy got together again, I felt happy for him, and maybe a little jealous.

"When I learned about the weird way Rick Ames intersected each of our lives, I felt angry at first, like that bastard had even wrecked a chance for Max to at last have a friend. What I'm sure Max hasn't told you—it makes him ashamed as much as angry—is there was a time when we were as good friends with Rick Ames and his-then wife as with anyone in the agency."

Max's head snapped up. "That's putting it a little stronger than I would."

"Maybe so, Max," she said, "but I think you know it's true."

"Don't feel you owe us any explanation, or need to say anything to make us feel better about that," Andy said. "I'm much more interested in making this time count for this friendship that came late and has become so precious to me."

"I'm about out of gas," Max said. His face betrayed a spasm of pain. "I'm going to suck down a semi-lethal dose of those OxyContin babies and take a nap. I'll be an hour, then we can talk more. Maybe you'd give me a hand getting out of this chair, Andy."

Andy got up and came around the table. He held out his hand. Max grasped hold, scrunched up his face and slowly pulled himself upright, groaning. He nearly pulled Andy down on top of him. He stood still for a moment, breathing hard.

"Whew, long way from diving into shark infested water in Iloilo."

Andy laughed. "You survived that. I dove in only because I was embarrassed not to after you did, but I figured it was the end of me. If sharks couldn't do you in, maybe cancer can't either."

Max smiled. "I understood sharks; can't say the same for cancer. I think I'm over matched this time."

"Can I give you a hand getting to your room?" Andy asked.

"Thanks, but no. I need to stop at the bathroom along the way, and so far I can still manage that on my own. When I can't, Morphine gets the nod."

"Now Max," Sandra protested, "this is trying enough without your getting maudlin."

Max didn't respond. He shuffled down the hall toward his bedroom.

Andy felt suddenly weary, defeated. "If you don't mind, Sandra," he said, "I think I might take myself back to your den and have a lie down on that big couch."

"Help yourself, Andy. Alice and I can tell secrets about you and Max."

"Help yourself," Andy said, as he went down the narrow hallway to the den. "My secrets have pretty much lost whatever interest they may once have had."

Alice helped Sandra clear the dishes, picking them up with the dish towel as Sandra put them in the drying rack. Sandra turned off the water, turned toward Alice.

"I'm glad we've got a few minutes alone," she said. There's something I want to say to you, to get off my chest."

Alice, towel in hand, looked curiously at Sandra. "Oh?"

Sandra strung out her words slowly, cautiously, "This Rick Ames thing isn't as straightforward as you may think. I fear you and Andy may be taking onto yourselves more than you deserve."

Alice hung the towel over the rack. "I never thought it was straightforward. Nothing about Rick ever was. And for lots of reasons, I think I feel worse than even Andy does about the havoc he wreaked, for us and for you. Though Andy sure feels stupid about it all now."

"Max can't think straight about it," Sandra said, fixing Alice with a stare that made her fidget. "But that's not only because of Rick turning out to be a double agent, which I think Max suspected for some time before he was caught."

Alice was silent, waiting for what Sandra might say next.

"You see..." Sandra began, then faltered, turned away. Alice reached for her, put her hand on her shoulder.

"When we were young, many Agency families lived close to each other in Arlington. Being in the same line of work and knowing our husbands couldn't tell us what they were doing made us a kind of secret society of our own." Sandra sighed a long, deep exhale.

"I was very drawn to Rick. Max and I were going through a particularly bad patch and Rick was getting divorced from his first wife."

Alice listened intently, trying to look more casual than she felt.

"It would be too dramatic to say we had an affair," Sandra said. "But it wouldn't be wrong to say we crossed a line. I only tell you this now because it isn't right for you and Andy to think all our upset falls on your friendship with Rick. But I'd just as soon you not let Max know I told you. It's maybe the sorest, unresolved issue between us. I can't ask you not to tell Andy but if you felt you didn't need to, I would be just as happy."

Sandra's shoulders drooped. Her head fell. She looked defeated.

"My God!" Alice said. "I just can't believe it."

"I'm afraid it's true," Sandra said.

"No, no," Alice explained, "not that. The lowest point in my marriage to Andy was when I came within an inch of having an affair with Rick. That man cut a wide swath."

Sandra stared at Alice, wide eyed. "How about a shot of vodka to calm the nerves?" Sandra asked.

"You're on."

Sandra reached into the cabinet over her head, bringing down two old fashioned glasses. She leaned over, opening the cabinet under the sink. She took out a fifth of vodka.

"Neat?"

"Neat," Alice answered. Sandra poured both glasses a quarter full.

"Here's to that miserable fucker being locked up forever for betraying more than just his country."

"I'll drink to that," Alice said, and she and Sandra held up their glasses, tapped them together, and each threw back her head and swallowed.

"Ooh," Alice exclaimed through her choking. "I've only ever seen that done in movies."

Sandra laughed. They embraced, holding it for a long time, laughing, crying.

"And here's to husbands getting old and needing naps so we can finally find enough time together to cut through the bullshit they seem to need to sustain their self-importance," Alice said.

A few minutes later Andy emerged from his nap, finding Alice and Sandra sitting at the kitchen table having an animated conversation.

"Looks like you two have found enough to entertain yourselves without Max and me," he said, thinking he sounded a little defensive. *It's always risky for men when women talk among themselves.*

"We've just been trading recipes," Sandra smiled. "Just discovering new ways to keep you boys happy."

Andy laughed. "Yeah, we do march like an army, on our stomachs. But happy? I used to long for it, now has hardly any meaning for me."

"That's depressing," Alice said. "What's eating you?"

"Oh, sorry, I didn't mean it to be. I think what I mean is more like content, than happy. Happy suggests a contrast with unhappy. Content is being OK with what is. Even pasta when you were hoping for caviar."

"You must have been dreaming in there," Alice said. "You came out full of something."

"Maybe it's discovering friends who are more than that— soul mates if that's not too corny. It's not just enough, it's pretty close to sublime. Not sure I was asleep at all but I had this sense that Julian of Norwich must have meant when she wrote: "All shall be well, and all manner of things shall be well."

"Sounds nice," Sandra said. "It would put most of us at the Agency out of business."

The three laughed.

"But it's not about the world becoming safe, or even OK," Andy explained. "It's about the occasional sense that nothing can happen to you that will erase the thrill, the wonder of just being here. And right after that piercing insight, you need to floss, or take a dump."

"Now there's an insight for the ages," Alice said.

"I appreciate what you said, Andy." Sandra said, "And I think I nearly understand it."

"Oh," Andy looked chagrined. "I hope I don't sound like I know what I'm talking about. I was just fumbling for words to describe what I was feeling while I was lying down just now. Almost an out of body thing, but I didn't leave my body or even feel like anything was really so different from normal.

"But when I came out and saw you two it was as if you had visited some place in the ether, had in some way been changed just in the time I was gone."

"You know something, there's a weird energy you two brought with you, Sandra said. "I think it's quite nice but it also feels a little scary. Challenging."

They were all silent, sitting at the table, looking down. Alice thought if Andy started in praying, or tried out more of his theology as he could when things got uncomfortable, she'd kick him in the groin. But he was still, quiet as she and Sandra were.

Sandra finally broke the silence. "I'm going to wake Max. He shouldn't miss all this happy hocus-pocus. And if he sleeps any longer he won't sleep a wink tonight. That means I don't sleep."

She got up and walked down the hall. Andy looked hard at Alice.

"Don't ask, Andy. Sandra is a lovely woman, and I'm so glad I came. We connected; that's all you need to know."

"Makes me happy, draws the amazing circle together, Alice."

They sat quietly for several minutes. Sandra came back down the hall to the kitchen, walking slowly, deliberately. She lowered herself into the chair next to Alice.

"He's gone," she said.

Andy and Alice looked at Sandra, then at each other.

"You mean…" Andy asked.

"Dead, lying on his back, mouth open, Sandra said. "I felt his carotid, put my ear to his mouth. Nothing. That's what that energy in the house was about. Max, leaving."

Andy got up and went to Sandra.

"Please don't hug me or anything just now, Andy. Max is pretty conventional about religion and so am I. He'd want you to go to him, pray, last rites. I'd like to go with you. Alice, too, if you will. But no tears, not yet. This is Max's doing. He knew. It's no coincidence that you're here."

The three of them rose from their chairs. Andy had to take hold of the counter to steady his wobbly legs. They walked down the hall side by side, bumping against each other awkwardly, not speaking. When they reached the bedroom Sandra went in first. Andy and Alice hesitated at the door, watching Sandra walk over beside the bed, kneel, and cup Max's still face in her hands. After a moment she looked over at them.

"Come," she whispered, gesturing with her head to the opposite side of the bed. Alice and Andy walked over and knelt beside Max's body, leaning on the bed to lower themselves onto their aging knees without falling onto his body.

After a long pause Sandra spoke. "This is his first moment without pain in more than 10 years." She looked over at Andy. And then she nodded to Andy.

Andy put his right hand onto the forehead of his oldest friend. It felt as warm as his own. He made the sign of the cross with his thumb.

"Unto God's gracious mercy and protection we commit you…"

~

CPSIA information can be obtained
at www.ICGtesting.com
Printed in the USA
LVOW11s1559041216
515740LV00001B/126/P